CREATORS OF EVIL: SIMPLY MURDERERS

By

Ambrocio Magaña Álvarez

Introduction

It is a nostalgic and terrifying book. It tells the story of a small ruthless being who, even before his birth, from his mother's womb, was already commanding his diabolical plan, which was to massacre an entire community and every living being that existed there, torturing them with severe punishments. Watching and hearing them beg for mercy was what amused him the most.

The other story is about a beautiful young woman who, from the very first breath in this life, already had her destiny written, which was to be very cruel and perverse, due to merciless people who condemned her to a cruel and miserable life, because of simple prejudices they held. They said she was responsible for all the misfortunes that occurred there. Everyone judged and condemned her. Because of that foolish prejudice, they accused her of being an evil and merciless witch, protected by Satan. That is why all the people who knew her united to try to massacre her. However, they did not succeed; she mysteriously disappeared, only to be found buried next to the grave of an old woman who had cared for her until her death when she was just a little girl. The mystery was that no one had buried her.

About the Author

I am from a very small community in the state of Michoacán, Mexico. I come from a large family of 12 siblings, and I am the seventh. I have very little formal education. I grew up in the countryside with peasant parents. As an adult, at the age of 20, I moved to California, USA, where I worked in the fields for 17 years, harvesting grapes, lemons, oranges, kiwis, apples, and pruning grapes, almonds, lemons, among others. After that, I went to Oregon to study in college, but due to my lack of English, I couldn't pass the classes and dropped out. I then moved to the state of Wisconsin, where I live with my wife, my daughters, and my son. I worked in factories until my retirement. That's why I now have time to try to make my dream come true, which is to be a writer of all kinds of books, of all genres, including humorous and other types of entertainment.

Table of Contents

LITTLE PRINCE OF EVIL

It is a story as sad as it is wicked, terrifying, chilling, full of fear, tragedy, pain, and suffering, which a community endured due to the curse of a small, ruthless, diabolical being. "YOU WILL BELIEVE ME" that from his mother's womb, he already unleashed the fury of his evil on that community, punishing them not only with a mocking laughter that echoed as he terrorized them but also cruelly massacred them without any mercy, even though his victims begged for it. For this prince of evil, watching them terrified and massacring them was what amused him the most.

FLOWERS FROM THE FIELD SHE GATHERED

This is very different from the other. It is about a precious young girl who, from birth, already had her curse written, which she would experience after arriving in this universe. From the tender age of five, she felt the contempt, insults, humiliation, fear, and perversity she was subjected to by the inhabitants of some communities, who, due to their foolish prejudices, judged and condemned her, believing she was an evil witch or the devil himself or had a pact with him, which is why he protected her when they tried to abuse or kill her. The hatred toward her was so great that they accused her of every tragedy that occurred in that community, blaming her for causing them. In the end, the beautiful young woman met an unpleasant, mysterious farewell to this world, as she was found buried next to the grave of an old woman who had cared for her when she was a child. The mystery was that no one had buried her.

LITTLE PRINCE OF EVIL

This is not a story, or rather, it wasn't a story, a legend, or a myth: **IT WAS A TRAGIC REALITY**. It was a terrifying, chilling, and ruthless reality, a cruel and inhuman massacre, an unwanted curse, an unpleasant encounter with the wickedness of a small evil being, a tormenting punishment. For just over three weeks, the residents of a town lived through something that, when you know the whole truth about it, you might think the same as I do. You'll say it's a joke, they want to pull my leg. But no, this was a cruel and wicked reality, a cruel evil wickedness that still today leaves scars and gruesome memories on the souls and bodies of those who lived and survived that horrible nightmare. Maybe you'll think that everything I'm going to tell you about the terrifying nightmare is a joke, and of the one who caused it, that while it was happening, people and all animals could hear the echo of his mocking, diabolical laughter. Hundreds of them are still true witnesses, with very visible marks on their souls and bodies from what that curse did to them, both people and animals, as they were being massacred. **WOULD YOU BELIEVE ME IF I TOLD YOU THAT HE WAS ALREADY COMMANDING HIS EVIL PLAN FROM HIS MOTHER'S WOMB?**

As I will tell you, it was no joke. The victims of that small evil being felt the pain, the suffering, a merciless punishment of being trapped by the curse, by the wickedness, watching others suffer the same as they did, crying out for help but being unable to help themselves, much less provide help to those who were imploring for it. When their cries of pleas, their last prayers, slowly stopped being heard, when their souls escaped from their bodies, unable to withstand the ferocious cruelty that massacred them, taking their lives without any compassion or mercy.

It is hard to believe when you're told something so wicked, something very regrettable, that when it began, no one could avoid becoming a victim of this curse, of that mortal nightmare, which now with great nostalgia, still leaves scars on the souls of all the survivors who can testify exactly how it began, how it started, how they were living it and how they lived through it. Dozens of people, and some animals that still exist, are visible witnesses of the gruesome tragedy, for they have indelible marks on their bodies from what they lived through. Just as hundreds could not withstand the demonic assaults of the fierce gales that, with the force of their fury, destroyed and massacred everything in their path.

That's why it's easy to believe that it's just a story to entertain or to fool those who listen, but no! **With my own eyes**, I could see part of what remains of that unpleasant tragedy, which still lingers among those who lived it and survived it, the clandestine graves of people and animals who paid with their lives for the tricks of that small diabolical being who came from hell itself to cause them suffering, terror, death, and the destruction of their homes and lives. These are the best witnesses, who preserve that unforgettable suffering, the story of that cursed moment.

Something I could never believe, and I don't think you are so skeptical as to think it's true, is when you're told a story that you didn't see happen or are presented with proof that it really did happen and where it happened. Because on these occasions, there are no witnesses or evidence to say it's true that it happened or that it could happen. **That's why** the cruel reality that was lived in that town may be very difficult for you to assimilate and think, yes, it was a ruthless, diabolical tragedy committed by a small evil creature. It's even harder to believe that from his mother's womb, he was already letting them feel the fury of the evil he came to do, and he had already warned them that very soon he would be among them.

Well: I know you won't believe me if I tell you that someone defended themselves with a little five-centimeter knife against twenty-five people carrying machetes and axes, that he didn't kill them, that just with that little knife, he knocked down the machetes and axes, and when he knocked them down, he grabbed them, tied them up, and piled them up until he finished with all of them. **Maybe you'd say** no, that's nothing, I know of someone else who defended themselves against forty warplanes that were launching missiles and atomic bombs at them, like a hundred per minute, and with just a cap, they knocked them off and sent them back until they defeated them all, knocking down some and scaring others away, making them flee. **Without a doubt, you won't believe it** but I will tell you something that I verified happened, a real tragedy that dozens of people told me about and dozens of animals that I could see also witnessed with their suffering. When they told me, I didn't believe it either; it was hard for me to assimilate it. That's why I took it upon myself to verify it. Let's see if you believe it, especially what a baby did before and just after being born. **If you don't believe it**, I hope at least you enjoy it, that it serves as a distraction. Remember that reading is culture! It helps you stop thinking about sad moments you've had, it helps you relax, it's an antibiotic against stress and bad moments you're going through, it might serve as a distraction, and you can share the joy of reading with your children or family.

I BEGIN TO DESCRIBE THE CURSE OR THE CHILLING REALITY THAT HAPPENED NOT MANY YEARS AGO IN A COMMUNITY OF ABOUT EIGHT HUNDRED TO A THOUSAND INHABITANTS, AS THERE ARE STILL PEOPLE AND LIVING BEINGS WHO ARE STILL WITNESSES OF THE FACTS, WHO SURVIVED THAT FATAL KILLER AND DISASTROUS ENCOUNTER WITH A SMALL WICKED, DIABOLICAL, AND EVIL BEING WHO ONLY CAME TO EARTH TO BRING THEM DISGRACE, DEATH, AND DESTRUCTION.

I will tell my story just as they told it to me and just as I could see part of what remains of the ruins of the disasters that were lived, just as I could see the suffering of dozens of people and animals who still bear that cross, which for them is cursed and heavy, just as with the pain they feel, they continue to endure it. Several of the still survivors, whose wounds on their bodies have not yet healed, say: **Only those who are no longer among them have erased them, and perhaps the next generations may have memories, as there are still marks that will make them remember for decades.**

They say, or rather they told me, that in that town where the chilling tragedy occurred, there was a very young, beautiful widow who was very well-known in the community. She was a widow; her husband had just died a few months earlier, but the woman was pregnant, giving birth to a beautiful baby a few months later. The child was so angelic that everyone admired him at the moment of his birth, saying that the little boy was very handsome, which is why he was admired by all who saw him.

They say she was always a woman very beloved by the entire community, and so was her husband. They were very kind, helpful people who helped everyone. **The woman**, upon becoming a widow, was very much appreciated by the entire community, which is why no one ever believed or even thought that they had anything to do with dark arts or demonic things. That's why no one ever thought or noticed anything strange in her behavior, much less believed that from the womb of that beautiful and kind woman whom the entire community appreciated, an evil baby would be born, capable of wanting to physically and morally destroy their lives, capable of wanting to destroy their peace, their faith, and their love for their religion, to shatter the lives of so many living beings that existed in that region.

It may be hard to believe what happened to them, according to those who saw the child born, those who, because of his beauty, called him "little prince" and others who also knew of his birth, who, although they did not see him born, knew of his arrival in this life. He was a child who seemed to be like any other, but those who had already seen him commented that he was as handsome and beautiful as a little prince. For everyone, he was the admiration of the community in that small village. What they never imagined was that this child, as handsome as a little prince, would be a prince of evil, a small being who would make them live the worst nightmare of their lives, provided they could withstand his wickedness. From before his birth, he brought destruction, pain, and death to their lives and to everything that lived there: people, horses, dogs, cows, and all kinds of animals. Everyone experienced, felt, and suffered something strange, something odd, some evil, something unknown that no one in that community had ever heard of happening. Today, no one can say that something like this happened in any other region or country, much less have suffered it.

All living beings in that town were living a nightmare. They didn't understand the evil that was massacring them, that curse that came like rain, like a wild wind, and along with this destruction came an epidemic of severe colds with coughs and strong chills with high fevers that formed due to the death of dozens of animals, which also made other animals sick and was the worst curse caused by the little prince. Together, they caused several human and animal losses. No matter how much they wanted to resist not dying, they were also victims of the merciless curse of that beautiful child, the prince of evil.

It's better I tell everything in detail as they told me, just as it happened, how they felt it, and how they lived it, all those who survived the fatal, bloody, malevolent tragedy of the little prince's wickedness.

It is said, or rather, those who told me, that about two weeks before the little prince was born, many strange things happened to people. They heard wolves howling inside their houses, strange noises everywhere they walked, and they heard them at all hours, wherever they were. But at night, they heard strange echoes of laughter that scared them and gave them chills. They could hear squeals like rats or a stuck boar, and there were fast winds that made them cold and frightened. People felt tired, fatigued; they looked like zombies to each other. They heard echoes of different noises and sounds that came from the hills, from all parts of the mountains.

They told me that strange aromas came with the wind, which was hard to understand and endure. The people couldn't avoid feeling them. The animals were also living the same nightmare, the same curse. They looked sad; their eyes were watery. Many didn't eat, the dogs and coyotes howled sadly, and the other animals spent almost the whole day sleeping as if they had been sick for several months. For everyone in the town, it was difficult to comprehend what was happening to them. They didn't want to be living that diabolical reality that was about to begin, the prank of the little prince of evil, who was just beginning to think about it as the start of the game he was going to show them.

They also told me that just before the week began, when the little prince was to be born, although it was daytime and sunny, it suddenly became cloudy and dark as if it were going to rain, but it didn't rain. It looked like a storm was coming, with hundreds of lightning bolts that almost killed people from how loud they were, but everyone thought it could be normal, that it was something happening with the changes nature was making. That's why no one suspected what might happen to them. They never imagined that that beautiful baby, watching them suffer, would be amused by it.

They also told me that just at the start of the week when the little prince was born, torrential merciless rains began to fall, lightning came, and with them, gusts of wind that almost seemed to speak from how loud they were. The townspeople, upon hearing the sound of the wind, said it seemed like a diabolical laugh mocking them. The strong winds destroyed houses and some trees, and the power had already been cut. The rivers were about to overflow from so much rain, and the scared people asked themselves what was happening. In previous years, they had experienced heavy downpours and unpleasant winds, but this time, they were more ruthless, crueler, and deadlier. People helped each other, searched for safer shelters, but each one was struck by the powerful winds that, with their force, were destroying them. That's when they realized they were about to suffer a tragedy. They were beginning to sense the terror they were going to live through. The scars on their bodies became visible, they helped each other, healed their wounds, gave each other courage to face the curse they were feeling. They thought they were suffering something that would be hard to forget for the rest of their lives, and just as they thought, it happened to them.

They told me that amidst the suffering, pain, and evil, no one could explain what was happening. Everyone wanted to know what was occurring, but no matter how much they asked, no one knew the answer. Even though they screamed, cried, and pleaded for mercy, there was nothing they could do to stop the fury of the cruelty they were experiencing. At that moment, some were already seeking answers from God, already asking Him for an explanation for what was happening to them, for what they were sensing would destroy them. With their eyes and the pain in their bodies and souls, they were witnesses that something sinister was about to change their lives, the lives of everything living there, but God did not seem to hear their pleas. Some were beginning to think that He had forgotten them.

They also told me that the dogs and cats hid under the beds, in the darkest corners they could find, howling as if something hurt them or as if they were being hanged or beaten. All the animals were restless, the chickens clucked fearfully, the cows and horses appeared sick, the roosters didn't crow, and no wild birds were seen flying. It was all hard to believe, but the hardest part was enduring the nightmare they were living, seeing the pain and terror on their faces from what they were suffering, without knowing how to help each other, the pain torturing them every passing second.

They told me that something tragic began to happen; there were already human losses to mourn. Some elderly people who had been a little sick worsened and died due to the cold winds, and dozens of animals drowned in the storms that were falling. There was a death toll among chickens, cows, donkeys, and other wild animals living nearby, which led to a severe epidemic of colds and coughs, as if they had tuberculosis, along with high fevers and chills that brought them to the brink of death, condemned to suffer. That's why they started to face what was happening, and despite the tragedy they were confronting, those who could do something found the strength to dig pits and bury nearly all the animals that had died and those that were still dying.

The pain and torment were so cruel and unbearable that some believers in God began to beg for everything to end, for the massacre to stop, so they could live their lives as before. But they were far from that answer because the little prince was just beginning to enjoy his happiness, his evil, the pleasure of destruction, and the immense satisfaction he got from making them suffer, from his wicked prank, the pride that had brought him there to that town, which a few days earlier seemed to be God's blessed land.

They told me that the people were extremely frightened, that many, in those days, were so fearful, anxious, panicked, and desperate that those who had the chance to flee left the town. But some died trying to escape from that place. They fled because they believed it was a cruel trick of the very devil, who wanted to destroy them and everything that still had life there. That's why he sent those disastrous rains, the abominable thunderclaps, along with those demonic winds that sought to destroy everything in their path.

Some told me that after seven days of such anguish and despair, everything seemed to have returned to calm, but that calm lasted only a few more hours, just for a day. A day when there was no wind, no noise, no sound of thunder, but it remained cloudy. The dogs came out of hiding, some chickens clucked, the roosters crowed, the few horses, donkeys, cows, and other animals ran through the pastures, and wild birds were seen flying again. Everything seemed to be back to normal, as if nothing had happened. Everyone was confident, just recounting their stories as if they were tales from centuries past, like in the times of the Inquisition, or like the readings in churches about how God sank Sodom and Gomorrah, or as other readings say, in the times of the floods, when only those who boarded Noah's Ark were saved.

They told me that after that brief respite given by the little prince, when everyone was calm, serene, and coming to terms with what had happened, all believing it had just been a dream, a bad nightmare of one night, that nothing had been real. But to their misfortune, it wasn't so. There came a moment when they heard the echo of mocking laughter, but they couldn't be sure where it came from, only that it penetrated their minds because, once again, the little prince had mocked them. He had only deceived them, played with their faith.

They told me that they tried to believe it was all over, that they had all dreamed the same thing, and that when they woke up, they said to themselves, thank goodness it was only a nightmare, that it was over. But they were far from reality because what the little prince had in store for them was only beginning. It was just the start of his prank, his fun, the pleasure of his destruction. He was just starting to smile at his game, and he was already preparing other schemes, barely beginning to move the chess pieces, just starting his practices and plans for how he wanted to torture them.

They told me they believed that, how unbelieving they were of the reality, because as it began to darken around eight in the evening, the dogs and cats started making the same whining sounds as if they were sick or being beaten. They hid again in the darkest places they could find. Other animals did the same, some stopped making noise, stopped running, and the wild birds were no longer seen flying. Everyone was scared and surprised, asking themselves the same question, and some were pleading with God for an answer, but God seemed not to be present. Only the devil, only Satan, was among them, watching them suffer, writhing in pain, seeing the cruel desperation on their faces because they couldn't withstand his wicked game, which had just begun. He wanted to humiliate them as much as possible, but then he wanted to massacre them because suddenly, they heard a terrible thunderclap. No one knew where it came from; it seemed the earth had opened up. Some people's ears burst, some later died from it, and others were left deaf. The impact was so tremendous that some houses collapsed, falling on top of them, injuring and killing some people, even some animals that were hiding.

They told me that along with that massacre, the disastrous winds returned, along with the demonic gusts of hateful lightning. The terrifying sounds caused some people to faint; they couldn't stay on their feet. The hailstorms were no exception; they returned with fury. People tried to help each other, the strongest ones trying to pull the wounded from the rubble to place them in safer spots. Others treated the wounded; some cried and knelt, others prayed where they lay, clutching crucifixes, rosaries, asking God, questioning what was happening.

They told me that many, amidst the rubble and the gusts of wind and rain, managed to get out as best they could. Desperate, they went to seek refuge in the church, the only place that seemed not to suffer from the evil that was happening there. All together, though some were very badly injured, barely able to speak, where they lay, sat, or knelt, fearing for their health and lives, they implored God for His blessing, mercy, and compassion, but there was no answer.

They told me that amidst the death and terror they were already living, the earth began to move, causing further destruction. People kept fainting while others helped the most injured, fighting not to give in so that their souls wouldn't escape, refusing to die. With the earth's movement, many animals came out of their hiding places, squealing in fear, looking for another place to hide. They too felt the fear of death, the dread of the cruelty they were experiencing. Stones broke away from the mountains, and the people were so desperate they couldn't do anything against that demonic curse. Worse still, a barrage of lightning struck for a long while, accompanied by torrential rain, strong winds, and hail the size of marbles, which massacred the already wounded survivors. The winds were so violent that they destroyed what was left of some houses, damaged some roofs, and with the violence of their fury, they destroyed trees and everything else in their path.

They told me that due to that disastrous fury and the weakness of some people who were already sick from the epidemic caused by the death of animals, more people lost their lives, along with other defenseless animals who fought not to die, not to lose the battle, not to be victims of the merciless cruelty of the little prince of evil, to which he had subjected them and seemed very pleased to do so, seeing the anguish and despair on their faces from the punishment he was giving them, a wicked punishment they didn't deserve to live through, much less pay with their lives the price he was imposing on them.

But because of the curse and their misfortune of having been born in that place, some, with their suffering and their lives, had to pay that wicked punishment. Those who survived did not fare well at all; to this day, they continue to pay for the cruelty they lived through, simply because they were in or had lived in the wrong place.

They told me that due to the death of animals, they had to create new cemeteries to bury the dozens of little animals that, unfortunately, continued to lose their lives due to the merciless destruction, to help somewhat with their salvation by preventing the epidemic from spreading indiscriminately. A few days before the tragedy began, they had been working on some constructions in that place, which was like the only blessing. They had machinery they used to dig the pits for the cemeteries where they were going to bury the animals that lost their lives due to the merciless curse. Thanks to the people who mustered the willpower, as best they could, even though badly injured, they helped drag or carry the dead animals to where they were going to be buried. Because of this, the epidemic did not worsen.

They told me that at that very moment, a mother was giving birth to a beautiful baby, and everyone believed that amid so much devastation, it was a blessing they were receiving. A new life was coming to take the place of others that were leaving this life, leaving this earth to become part of it because they couldn't withstand the storms or the savage aggression of that beautiful child who had just arrived among them, without them realizing that he was the cause of the misfortune they were experiencing. Even before his birth, he unleashed his fury on them, with no mercy or way for them to defend themselves or prevent what happened.

They told me that many people thought that after everything, something good was happening, that there was something more to tell, but in their innocence, they didn't realize that the birth of that child was the nightmare they were living. That child was responsible for the curse they were suffering, for the massacre they were enduring. Some people, due to the relentless destruction, had already died; hundreds of little animals had stopped breathing the air of that beautiful nature they inhabited. They already had the dead to mourn and bury, dozens of wounded to heal and care for, and hundreds of animals that had died and been buried, while others were dragged away by the water currents that formed in the streets of that town, still suffering and dying.

They told me that the child was so beautiful that everyone who saw him was happy because he seemed strong and healthy. When they saw him, they said he was very handsome, like a little prince. It was like a miracle that he had been born without any complications and was healthy. And above all, his house was the only one untouched by the disastrous curse; it was intact, making it seem unreal what was happening in that town, that both he and his mother were in good health.

They told me that the little prince's birth was normal, that his mother had no complications, and that they were not suffering from the curse that everyone else was experiencing. But indeed, a beautiful child was born, a little prince, but a prince of evil, one they would all remember for the rest of their lives, leaving marks for others who would live or visit that place.

They told me that he didn't cry when he was born, only made some whimpers and sneezes, something that every baby normally does. But the person who helped him be born felt that he was very warm, though they thought it was normal, so no one was surprised, no one sensed or suspected that the child who had come into this world was not human, but Satan himself, disguised as a beautiful baby, who had come from the very depths of hell to destroy their faith and happiness. Everyone said he was an angel, "Yes, an angel, but of the devil."

They told me that about six hours after the little prince was born, they noticed him yawn. Some people who had just arrived to visit him saw his tongue, round with two pointed tips like a snake's, something neither his mother nor the woman who helped him be born had noticed. But the people who had just arrived and saw him were surprised and made fun of him. The little prince threw a strange tantrum, as if he understood that they were mocking him. The mother, without malice, told them not to make fun of him because God would punish them. When the mother mentioned God, the little prince opened his eyes and had another strange tantrum, his eyes bulging, and they saw that his eyes were the color of fire, almost like congealed blood mixed with ash.

They told me that no one could tell if he was born that way or if it happened later, and the people, in their innocence, continued to mock him. The little prince kept throwing strange tantrums when suddenly, the people who mocked him felt dizzy. They didn't pay much attention to it, but they began to feel hot and simultaneously experienced chills, sweating an unbearable odor. That's why they had to leave that place, and by morning, they saw their skin darkening, like the color of coal with ash.

They told me that they became so pale and weak that they didn't understand what was happening. The chills and fevers were cruel and painful, making them delirious and scream in pain. The torment they were feeling was unbearable, and they desperately begged for help from others and mercy from God. Some people wanted to help them but didn't know how or had no medicine to give them. They didn't know what to do for them. Everyone could see their anguish, how they felt, how they cried out in pain. Some tried to comfort them, telling them that everything would pass, to have faith, that God was with them, that they were not alone, and that soon they would regain their health and peace.

They told me that when night fell, it didn't stop raining or lightning, and the turbulent, terrifying thunder didn't stop. The destruction continued; more people and animals were getting infected and dying from the epidemic and destruction, with no end in sight. The rivers, swollen by the storms, had exceeded their capacity.

They told me that the river currents dragged animals, horses, donkeys, cows, and more, some dead and some alive, with some poor creatures struggling for their lives amid the wild currents, seemingly asking for help, hoping someone would rescue them. But unfortunately, the people were in the same situation, fearing for their lives, pleading for mercy from God, and watching the animals drown, seeing them suffer without being able to help.

The people who were living through this or who had the chance to know about it said it was something incredibly difficult to believe, something unimaginable. That's why they said they didn't understand what was happening to them. The incredible thing was that, despite the two rivers in the town overflowing with water, just a few kilometers outside the town, they seemed to dry up. The water evaporated as if the currents carrying everything in their path were just soap bubbles or cotton candy sold at fairs, easily disintegrating in the air or sun. The cruelty of their macabre disaster did not reach other towns that were just about thirty kilometers away.

They told me that the people no longer had any doubt that Satan was among them, that he was the only one responsible for their curse, for the misfortune they were experiencing, and that the punishment they were receiving was something only they deserved. They noticed that the rivers, despite their immense fury when they passed through the town and reached other communities not far from there, were normal, like in other times of heavy rain. It seemed like the work of God or that the curse of the beautiful little prince was only for that town and that they alone had to pay the price that the newly arrived beautiful little prince wanted them to pay.

They told me that even today, there are dams along the river from that town to nearby ones, dozens of them filled with the bones of hundreds of little animals that were dragged and massacred by the fury of the currents. I was able to verify this during my visit, and it wasn't a lie; it had been a true massacre, a cruel nightmare that those little animals couldn't endure. With their noble lives, they too had to pay the price for the happiness the little prince felt as he watched them suffer the cruelties he was bestowing upon them, the torture, the punishment, the pain, just to feel the pleasure of seeing them fade away, watching their last breaths escape, their souls leaving their bodies. Perhaps that was his mission on this earth, to enjoy seeing people and thousands of living beings suffer and then, after his fun, to take their lives.

They told me that people believed it was the work of the devil, that the devil was loose among them. Some people seemed to be losing their faith in God, starting to think that God had abandoned them, which is why Satan had unleashed such evil against them. Some people began to suspect the little prince, questioning why nothing happened in his house. They realized that the people who got sick after seeing him at birth were still suffering from the same symptoms they felt when they mocked the beautiful child, that beautiful little prince, the prince of evil. That's why some people started murmuring that he could be the cause of all the evil, the misfortune they were experiencing, but it was difficult to be sure. And so, with that anguish, with unanswered questions, terrified in their suffering, they had to continue with their lives.

They told me that those who cared for the mother and the little prince said that nothing happened inside that house, that they didn't feel the fearful thunder of lightning or the savage, merciless winds. They saw the little prince throw tantrums, get angry, and it seemed that only when he was outside the house did the merciless rains, the atrocious sounds of thunder, and the fury of the winds grow stronger. It seemed they could hear a disturbing laugh that gnawed at their ears, mocking them, with diabolical echoes of the devil himself. The people, the wounded, the sick with the epidemic, cried and prayed, begging God for forgiveness if they had offended Him in any way, pleading for His mercy and compassion, for the mistakes they had made or the harm they had done or caused. Terrified in their suffering and pain, they screamed that they didn't deserve what they were going through, that it was too cruel what they were experiencing, crying out to God, "If it isn't You punishing us, please help us." They cried, "If it is the devil who wants to end our lives, for mercy or compassion, stop him."

They told me that not only were the people terrified, but the few animals still resisting the attacks of their suffering stayed in their hiding places if they could. Others wandered around in fear, not knowing where to go or where to hide, as the little prince's fury also took pleasure in watching them suffer, and after satisfying his desire, cowardly taking their lives without any compassion, just as he was enjoying it with the people. It was an honor for him to see them suffer, to beg for their lives, and then to massacre them.

They told me that as the days passed, everyone believed that yes, that beautiful child who had just arrived among them was indeed the devil himself, in the body of that baby, who some thought was harmless. But with some events that seemed to be confirmed, they believed that the little prince was the real culprit for their tragedy, as it seemed very incredible and strange that only that house hadn't suffered any damage, and when the little prince cried or threw his tantrums, something sinister, something terrifying was about to happen. Another little mischief had occurred to that precious child. They also believed that the church, despite the devastation of other buildings, remained intact, not destroyed. That's why they believed the devil was among them, only to unleash the fury of his wickedness on them, with no way to stop him. Everyone believed that only a miracle from God could stop him from massacring them any further, from destroying their lives and their faith.

They told me that as night fell, the terrified people kept asking themselves what they had done to deserve such a cruel punishment. They asked themselves a thousand times how to escape the massacre, the nightmare that was ending them, how to help one another, how to return to their normal lives without pain or tears, how to protect the animals who also sought protection. But how could they protect them if the people themselves couldn't help each other because of what they were feeling? No one could help them, and how could they heal the wounds that were bleeding, how to cure the epidemic they were suffering from when they had no medicine for the epidemic or to treat the wounded? That's why they couldn't help others, why they were clamoring for help, everything that had life there was suffering from the curse of the little prince.

They told me that the prayers and pleas didn't cease, that they continued amidst the people's sobs. Without mercy, the hateful thunder and strong winds, the rains, and hail continued. The panic and terror among the people remained, with no compassion from the merciless curse of the little prince of evil. The wickedness continued, but the people had faith that God would rescue them. In their cruel suffering, they clung to not being defeated. Yet for some, it was difficult to endure. Deep down, their souls burned with pain, but they didn't want to give up. They felt the faith that would return their happiness, that all that evil would be forgotten from their minds. That's why they kept asking for clemency or compassion from God to rescue them from Satan's claws, who didn't want to stop torturing them. The celebration, the fun for the wicked child of evil, the little prince of evil, wasn't over yet. Perhaps it was too much fun for him to see them wounded, crying, and suffering, not wanting to stop torturing them. His desire was to mock them and then take their lives without any compassion.

They say that faith moves mountains, and that God made the mountains, that only He could destroy them. That town with faith in God was like the mountains, that only He could destroy it. But Satan wanted to win the battle, to strip Him of His believers. That's why he had come ahead before their faith could spread to other towns where Satan was already the master and lord. That's why in other towns, crimes, child abuse, mistreatment of the elderly and disabled, cruelty to animals, destruction of nature, along with alcohol and drugs, were present every day.

They told me that as the night passed, the people in the church, others in their homes, remained terrified in that destroyed place. Just when dawn began, they saw a light at the edge of the town, like a rainbow, coming closer and closer to them until it reached the church, where many of the sick and wounded were. A few minutes later, some people saw that among the rain, the debris in the battered streets left by the strong winds and torrential downpours, they saw an unknown woman, tall and thin, a bit disheveled, stumbling and getting up among the puddles, debris, and mud, approaching them.

One of the survivors of the merciless tragedy told me that just when they saw the woman, the rainbow light disappeared. Some people said that although the woman fell and got up, her clothes didn't get dirty, and when she approached them, the sun began to emerge, and the thunderous lightning and savage winds ceased for a moment. They saw the sun come out, but the people were still astonished; they couldn't stop crying and praying, blessing each other with crucifixes, as if driving Satan away. That's why no one offered the woman help, no one knew who she was, because no one asked her or she didn't ask them what was happening or if there was anything she could do to help. Although they believed the woman was the one coming for help, they didn't realize that she was the help they had been desperately pleading for in their delirious prayers.

They told me that the woman appeared to be elderly, and they believed she was either God or a celestial angel sent to them because she didn't speak to anyone or look at anyone. As if she already knew where the little prince was, she approached the door, and as if she lived there, she opened it and entered the house. When she opened the door, some told me that a foul odor, like burnt leather and oil mixed with garbage, filled the air. As the smell emerged from the house where the little prince was, it became difficult for the people nearby to endure, so some decided to distance themselves from that place.

Her faith was infinite because after this woman's visit, they believed they had received another blessing: despite the disastrous storms and destructive winds, along with the terrifying thunder, from that day on, no pregnant woman or female animals lost their babies or had any complications during childbirth, despite the epidemic that had been trying to wipe them out.

They told me that some curious onlookers, peering through the cracks in the house, saw the woman speaking to the mother, seemingly asking for permission to bless her child. It was as if the mother had also sensed that her son had something to do with the tragedy occurring outside their home, so she agreed to the mysterious woman's request.

Those who were watching said that the woman placed a rosary around the baby's neck, but when the little prince felt it on his chest, he twisted like a small snake and let out a cry similar to that of rats or a trapped boar. This frightened the woman, and she dropped the rosary to the floor. Trembling as if in fear and looking at the little prince, she bent down to pick it up, but it seemed as though it burned her hand, as if she had grabbed a burning ember. She tried to throw it onto the little prince's chest, but it didn't land on him; it fell to the floor again. The woman appeared terrified and picked it up, only for it to fall once more.

They told me that the woman was shaking with fear, looking as though she thought the little prince might attack her. She seemed to be terrified of him. She bent down again to pick up the rosary from the floor, but she was so shocked that she didn't want to put it on him again. That's why people believed she was either God, a celestial angel sent by God, or that the woman was also a believer in both God and the devil, and that's why she came to help, to try to calm the forces of Satan's evil. But it seemed that Satan was deeply embedded in that little baby's body, and she believed no one could drive him out—it was difficult to control.

They told me they saw the woman freeze for a moment, pressing her head with her hands, staring at the little prince, as if a thought had suddenly come to her. She got the idea to bathe him and then asked the mother for permission to do so, which the mother granted. She wrapped the little prince in a towel, picked him up in her arms, and took him to another room, where she stayed alone with him.

They told me that the curious onlookers heard the woman talking to herself. They heard her say that he was heavy and very hot, which wasn't normal for a baby. Once she had the little prince in her arms, she locked herself in a room so that no one could see them. She laid him on an old bed, but some curious people still managed to peek through any hole or crack they could find.

They told me that they believe she sprinkled him with holy water because they saw her take a bottle out of her clothes and open it, pouring the water onto his body. But when the water touched the little prince, they saw him twist like a snake, stick out his tongue, and his eyes bulged. They heard a squeal like that of rats or a trapped boar coming from the little prince as the water hit him, and once again, a strange, foul odor emanated from the house, so disgusting that some people felt like vomiting, while others decided to leave the place. They said that the woman helping him could barely stand the stench that the little prince was emitting from his body or his breath, so she decided to leave.

They told me that the woman, shocked, looked at the little prince, covered him with a towel, and then picked him up in her arms. Still very frightened, she hurried out of the room, holding the little prince, who continued to writhe in her arms as if trying to escape. She seemed to grip him tightly so that he wouldn't fall, leaving the little prince next to his mother, and only said, "I will return later." The little prince's mother was so surprised that she couldn't even ask the woman what was happening to her son. The woman rushed out of the house, almost running, and they heard her muttering, "I need help, I need help because the devil is here." They saw that mysterious woman leave through the same destroyed streets by which she had arrived, walking until she disappeared into the forest. They noticed that she was no longer dirty, didn't slip in the debris or stagnant water, and didn't fall, which made those who stayed behind believe she was indeed sent by God.

They told me that when they could no longer see the woman, as she walked down the riverbank and out of sight, the cruelty of the gusting winds, the terrifying thunder, and the hail returned mercilessly, destroying more and more. It seemed as if they could hear diabolical laughter in their minds, not knowing where it came from, as if the little prince believed he had won the battle and was mocking the mysterious woman too, believing he had defeated her. That's why the little prince, with a diabolical laugh, wanted to continue torturing them; his game was just getting started, far from over.

They say that the prayers of the sick and wounded continued throughout that day and night because their faith and hope that God would hear them was unwavering. They believed that God, in the form of that woman, had visited them, and their faith was unshakeable. Even though they seemed defeated, it was difficult to extinguish their faith—it never wavered. They said that no matter how much Satan made them suffer or tortured them, he couldn't take away their faith in God, that God was more powerful, and that He would triumph over good and evil. The devil would not mock God and their faith.

Everyone who was there believes that the woman was indeed God, or as they began to say, an angel sent by Him, transformed into that strange, slender woman or a messenger sent to show them that He had not abandoned them. That's why she left, perhaps to seek help from a nearby place or from her heavenly Father, because at dawn, amid the destruction of the cruel rains, merciless winds, and the light of terrifying lightning, along the same streets and riverbank where the mysterious woman had appeared, they saw a priest approaching on horseback. He was slowly coming towards them, and without saying anything to anyone, he dismounted in front of the little prince's house. Like the woman, as if he already knew why he was there, he opened the door to the little prince's house and entered, as if he lived there. Once again, when the door opened, a fatal, unbearable stench emanated from the little prince's house.

They told me that when the priest opened the door, as if he already knew what was happening, he went straight to the little prince and his mother's room. When the priest opened the door, he felt something strange and sensed that the newborn was not a normal child but rather the devil, transformed into a little prince—a beautiful child that everyone admired. That's why he decided to ask the mother for permission to make the sign of the cross and bless the child. The mother, being a believer in God, agreed.

They said that the priest blessed him and made the sign of the cross with a crucifix he held in his hand. As he did so, he saw the little prince's eyes bulge, and he stuck out his tongue like a snake. But some curious onlookers noticed something strange about the priest—they saw that he seemed tense and scared, as if he was beginning to sweat. Without asking the mother, he took the little prince in his hands and entered the same room where the mysterious woman had locked herself in earlier. He closed the door and immediately began sprinkling holy water over the little prince's entire body, praying in a strange way, as if in a language only he knew.

They say that some people heard the little prince crying, squealing non-stop like rats fighting or a trapped boar, writhing worse than a snake burning when the holy water touched his body. The priest struggled to hold him, as if the little prince was trying to fall off the old bed, fighting him off. Outside, the gusts of terrifying thunder increased, the rain grew stronger, and the fierce winds destroyed what little remained of the devastated community. This was a town where, weeks before, people had been peaceful and happy, but that day they were living the worst nightmare, the hardest pain to endure, the worst massacre of their lives, the worst epidemic, the worst curse they had ever experienced.

They told me that due to the disastrous winds and the hateful thunder, some people fainted, and there were more deaths to mourn—they couldn't withstand the impact of the merciless curse. The destruction was even more savage than before, and the streets seemed like rivers from the flooding caused by the relentless rains, further destroying the community.

They say that the strongest among them could barely drag the fainted people out and rescue the dead from the water currents and the rubble of collapsed houses. It was difficult to carry the wounded to safer places where someone could take care of them, although it was nearly impossible to find them, as most of the homes were almost entirely destroyed.

They told me that they saw the priest looking helpless against the little prince. The priest was sweating and appeared exhausted because he couldn't control him, and his prayers in different languages only made the little prince more rebellious. The little prince nearly stood up as he squealed, seemingly wanting to fight back, to defend himself with bites and scratches, as if trying to rid himself of the priest to stop him from blessing or bothering him any further.

They told me that they saw the priest growing angry and frustrated. Desperately, he grabbed the little prince roughly, half-wrapped him in a towel, and took him back to his mother's room, leaving him there with her. The priest, seemingly frightened or desperate, told the mother, "I can't understand what's happening. I'm leaving, but I'll be back." Once again, the mother was left stunned, unable to even murmur or ask anything.

Some people told me that as the priest left the little prince's house, they heard him muttering, and suddenly, they heard him say, "The devil is here; I need help." They also heard him recall that in the nearby town, they were holding patronal masses, offering them to some saints of the community, with two bishops and a cardinal present. Amid the tears, prayers of the fainted people, thunder, rain, and the destructive winds, the priest mounted his horse. Everyone watched as he slowly rode away through the cruel destruction, down the same streets and riverbank where the mysterious woman, believed to be God or an angel sent to them, had arrived. The priest left without saying a word, and once he was out of sight, they heard a new mocking laugh, accompanied by the thunderous claps and fierce winds. It was as if that precious baby was celebrating his triumph with cries of happiness, having defeated a new rival.

They told me that the next day, just before dawn, they felt a sense of relief, as if they were healing from the epidemic and their wounds, because the hateful thunder and destructive winds slowly began to subside. They were no longer as fierce and destructive as they had been just a few hours earlier. For the desperate inhabitants of that town, it felt like another miracle, that at least for a few minutes, Satan had stopped massacring them and mocking them. That's why they were now certain that God was with them, because at that very moment, amid the diminished rain and destructive winds, some people saw that along the riverbank, through the same streets where the woman of God and the priest had come, they could see the priest returning, accompanied by two bishops and a cardinal, all on horseback.

They told me that when the priest, the two bishops, and the cardinal arrived, they dismounted from their horses in front of the little prince's house without saying a word or greeting anyone. They approached the house as if they lived there, opened the door, and went straight to the room of the little prince and his mother. Once again, an unbearable, stinking odor emanated from the house. After entering, they closed the door so that no one could hear or see what was happening. Some people approached the door, and others, out of curiosity, peeked through the cracks in the walls to see and hear what was going on.

They told me that through the cracks in the door and walls, they saw the priest, the two bishops, and the cardinal asking the mother for permission to do what they needed to do. The mother told them to go ahead. Those who were watching believed that the mother was beginning to accept that her son was indeed responsible for the curse, that she had given birth to a little demon, not the normal baby she had expected. That's why she didn't refuse to let them bless him or bathe him in holy water.

They told me that some of those who watched saw the Cardinal take the little prince to the same room where the Priest had previously tried to expel the demon from his soul. He laid the little prince on the same old bed, and as soon as the Cardinal touched him, the little prince twisted and almost fell to the floor. He began to scream, and those who were watching said that the Priest, the two Bishops, and the Cardinal quickly, as if terrified, began to bless him with holy water. The four of them held him down as if restraining a very strong person they needed to subdue. They began speaking or praying in what seemed like another language, blessing the little prince with their hands and crucifixes, performing an exorcism.

They told me that the onlookers watched the religious figures, but suddenly, all the onlookers began to hear different voices and shrill, unbearable noises, difficult to endure. At the same time, they began to feel nauseous, some even vomiting because of the smoke and the unbearable stench emanating from the little prince's house. The smell was so foul, like burning trash mixed with oil and leather, that some people left, unable to endure it, while others decided to stay to be sure that these religious men were indeed sent by the woman, like soldiers of battle sent by God to defeat Satan, who wanted to take control of the town's people.

Some of those watching the Priest, the two Bishops, and the Cardinal blessing the little prince also saw the mother locked in her room. She was very desperate, appearing confused, and she seemed to start believing that her son was not human but the devil himself, who had been conceived within her and came to earth through her only to cause the evil that was happening outside her home. She was very confused, unable to believe that she was the instrument Satan used for one of his most macabre, deadly, and disastrous punishments on that humble community, which had only weeks before enjoyed a peaceful harmony, so unlike the cruel reality they were now living. She herself believed it was a terrible massacre that the town was enduring.

They told me that throughout the town, amid the foul smell, the destructive rains, and the demonic lightning, they felt an earthquake as if the mountain had collapsed and the ground had opened up. Some people fell to the ground from the terrifying sound that shook the few houses still standing against the little prince's devastating curse. Some people's eardrums burst from the strong impact, causing them to lose their lives.

They also told me that severely wounded and terrified people tried to help each other, reviving one another, saying, "God is with us; He will save us from this massacre." Some of the stronger individuals helped the fainted ones to safer places and carried the wounded to the nearest houses that were not as badly damaged. Others took refuge in the church, which was barely holding up against the evil sounds of the demonic lightning and the disastrous winds, amid the debris left by the bloody earthquake that had just struck.

They told me that amidst the horror of the destruction, among the dead, the healthier survivors, those who resisted the evil, the stronger ones were helping each other. You could hear the cries of children and older people, and their pleas and prayers to God were repeated endlessly in their mouths, asking Him to bless them. Suddenly, a very bright light, like a comet or the flare of a rocket, was seen, but it didn't make a sound. It lasted for a moment, illuminating the entire village, and they could see that the ground had not split, and the mountains had not crumbled.

They said the survivors were stunned by what they were seeing, even more so because the ground hadn't split, and the mountains hadn't been destroyed. But they continued to cry, perhaps out of pain or joy, from the overwhelming suffering they were enduring or simply from not understanding what was happening. They only knew they were in danger, being cruelly wounded and massacred.

They told me that the light wasn't like lightning, but rather as if the sky had exploded, and then something even stranger happened—about twenty minutes later, the rain, hail, lightning, and strong wind began to calm down little by little. At that moment, some people took the opportunity to repair or reinforce their houses so that the demonic winds wouldn't carry them away. Meanwhile, others continued to watch and listen to the Priest, the two Bishops, and the Cardinal, speaking or praying in what seemed like another language that only they understood. Through the cracks in the house, they saw the little prince writhing and screaming in their hands, uncontrollable. The foul stench from the little prince began to spread throughout the destroyed village, and those who were closest had to cover their noses and mouths. Some left because they couldn't bear the stench without vomiting.

They told me that the smell kept coming, like burning leather, oil, and trash. Suddenly, when the sky was almost clear, more clouds formed quickly, the rain became denser, and the lightning more rapid and loathsome. Even so, for a short time, the curious onlookers peeking through the cracks saw that the Priest, the two Bishops, and the Cardinal looked tired and sweaty, as if they were in a desert or doing strenuous exercise. They could hear how loudly the little prince screamed and writhed as they prayed over him and sprinkled him with holy water all over his body, placing crucifixes on his chest and forehead.

They told me that they saw the little prince's eyes bulging, his body swelling and turning a dark purple. The Priest, the two Bishops, and the Cardinal appeared even more exhausted and sweaty, almost as if they were going to faint. But they encouraged each other, saying, "We must not give up; we have to defeat the demon. There are four of us and only one of him; we have more power; we must defeat him. He must not mock us."

Meanwhile, outside, almost everyone was still complaining, tending to each other, helping one another, or burying some of the dead people and animals that had perished. Some animals were already decomposing, and it was dangerous to keep them there, as they could spread the epidemic. Outside, the nightmare of the curse continued.

Some told me that inside the little prince's house, the Priest, the two Bishops, and the Cardinal were performing prayers and exorcisms. The little prince was swelling even more, like a toad when it gets angry, and suddenly, he lifted his body like an adult trying to sit or stand up. While in a sitting position, he let out horrible groans, throwing punches, biting, scratching, and suddenly sneezing violently. With great force, he exploded, showering them with his foul-smelling blood as he burst. Almost simultaneously, they all fell backward to the ground and quickly began wiping the blood off their faces and robes with whatever they could find. The little prince fell back onto the old bed at the moment of the explosion.

They told me that nearly fainting, the Priest, the two Bishops, and the Cardinal saw a very strange, monstrous creature about twenty centimeters tall emerge from the little prince's stomach. It resembled a goat standing on its hind legs but had the face of a hairless wolf with rat-like ears. They saw that it had no hair or tail and had two long beards. They also noticed that its eyes were bulging and bleeding. It jumped to the floor, and the Priest, the two Bishops, and the Cardinal tried to catch it, but due to their weakness, they couldn't. The creature slithered out like a burning snake, screaming and raging, through the cracks in the door, running away.

They told me that outside, some onlookers also tried to catch it with clubs, but it jumped like a kangaroo rat, too fast for them to hit. They couldn't stop it. Then they saw it in the flashes of lightning as it entered the river, and as soon as it felt the cold water, it squealed, not like a boar but like a flock of crows and other strange noises. The onlookers shouted and criticized it, seeing the monster that had come out of the little prince's stomach cross the river without stopping its squealing and foul stench, even though the current was strong, it wasn't swept away.

They told me that people kept covering their noses and mouths because the creature that emerged from the little prince's stomach left its foul stench for a long time. Even after it crossed the river, they continued to hear the squealing until it seemed to disappear far off into the mountains.

They told me that some people saw the Priest, the two Bishops, and the Cardinal begin to recover, although they could barely move, walk, or stand. They didn't stop praying and saw the little prince lying there, seemingly dead, only making weak groans with different sounds. But he hardly moved, his eyes still bulging. They looked at each other and nodded, realizing they were still covered in the foul blood that had sprayed from the little prince when he exploded. They couldn't bear the stench, so they quickly changed out of their clothes and into others they had fortunately brought with them.

Some people told me that the religious men observed the little prince again and saw that he was fine. They seemed to agree, exclaiming, "We did it! We defeated him!" They raised their hands as if wanting to dance, and despite their exhaustion, they almost fell over with joy and hugged each other in celebration, shouting, "We defeated him! We beat Satan! The little prince is safe!" They saw that the little prince was no longer screaming or writhing as he had before exploding or before the demon escaped from his body. They covered him with a cloak they had brought, noting that he no longer smelled as bad, but his stomach was still bleeding.

One of the people who witnessed what happened told me that after a brief celebration by the religious men, they sat down on the old bed next to the little prince. They looked extremely tired, as if they were asleep while sitting; they didn't move or talk. They remained like that for about five minutes, and when they seemed to wake up, they looked at each other, smiled, and stood up. The witness couldn't hear what they said because they spoke in low voices, but they saw them nod their heads as if saying, "We defeated him, let's go." The Priest picked up the little prince and took him back to his mother.

They told me that the Priest, the two Bishops, and the Cardinal explained to the mother everything they had done with her son and everything that had happened. The woman was very tense, very scared, trembling as she sighed deeply and cried. She said she had already sensed that something strange was going to happen and that she had hoped the demon would be expelled from her son's soul but not in the form of an animal, and that it would allow itself to be seen and run away like an animal, without being caught. The Cardinal responded, saying that it was the demon, and it wouldn't allow itself to be caught.

They told me that the onlookers who had been listening to the religious men's explanation to the mother dared to open the door to tell them that they had also seen it when it left through a crack in the house. They tried to catch it, but they couldn't either, as it jumped very quickly and strangely. They didn't imagine it was the demon; they only thought it was a very strange animal that might have come from the countryside seeking refuge, possibly fleeing out of fear.

They also told me that after the religious men and the onlookers shared what had happened, they noticed that the mother of the little prince was very sad and confused. She said that thanks to them, her son had been freed from the cruel perversity he was living in, and she was suffering too, seeing and hearing her son while they were helping to expel Satan from his body and soul. She repeatedly, through tears, thanked the religious men for saving her son from the devil's clutches, who had come from hell only to bring misfortune, to try to destroy the faith and peace of her son, herself, and the entire community. She said she was not a believer in any kind of witchcraft, spell, or satanic belief that would allow the devil to be conceived in her body. Even more disconcerting, to her surprise and everyone else's, was the idea that the demon could have entered her and her son's soul but not their bodies in the form of an animal. With great distrust and uncertainty toward the religious men and those who had lived through that incredible and disturbing moment, the mother asked for forgiveness on behalf of herself and her son, making it clear that neither she nor her son were guilty.

They told me that the people who witnessed the event didn't seem to accept the mother's apologies, but even so, they didn't say anything. Only the religious men seemed to understand what had happened, saying that on many occasions, in one way or another, they had already fought against Satan. But the way Satan had manifested this time was something they had never experienced. It was difficult for them to accept the way he had hidden within the bodies of the mother and the little prince in the form of a very strange animal. The Priest, the two Bishops, and the Cardinal said that Satan was very cunning and that nothing good could ever be expected from him.

The mother, terrified by what had happened, realized that she had been a satanic instrument, allowing the demon to take possession of her son's body and come to destroy the town. Although the town wasn't completely annihilated, it did suffer the massacre of hundreds of human lives, thousands of domestic and wild animals, and the near-total destruction of homes. However, for the mother and the religious figures, the important thing was that after all their efforts, they managed to banish the demon that had possessed the womb of that kind woman, inhabiting the body of that beautiful baby, who, once freed from the demon, seemed to be a normal baby after all.

They told me that the religious men looked so exhausted that it seemed as if they had been stranded in a desert for three days without food or water. They appeared very weak, but they could smile as they spoke, though it was still difficult for them to pronounce words without effort. Nevertheless, they were celebrating the battle they had won against the demon, which had required tremendous effort, and at the same time, they had restored the faith of the surviving inhabitants of that town. They also set an example for other believers, showing that when there is faith in God, anything can be achieved. EVERYTHING CAN BE ACCOMPLISHED.

They told me that the religious men considered leaving the house, but not before blessing the woman and the little prince. After placing the baby next to his mother, the little prince no longer screamed or threw a tantrum. He didn't cry, and the mother, the Priest, the two Bishops, and the Cardinal, along with others who had witnessed the terrifying scene inside the house, saw that the baby only opened his eyes. They noticed that his eyes were no longer red like congealed blood and ash; then they saw him yawn, and they observed that his tongue was also normal, like any other child's. They told the mother that she could be more at ease now because the demon was no longer within her son, and he was now a normal child.

They told me that both the religious men and the onlookers, all smiling and proud of their work, believed that everything had finally ended. They looked at each other, still appearing very tired, as if they were on the verge of falling asleep. But their smiles showed that they were very happy. Exhausted, they sat on the bed next to the little prince and his mother. Some of the others in the room also looked for a place to sit, but they still felt a sense of fear that nothing was certain, even though the religious men had assured them. The feeling of uncertainty lingered in their hearts, still too recent for them to fully believe it and feel confident in the reality that it would never happen again.

They told me that at that moment, someone arrived asking for help from the religious men, as some people were dying and wanted to see the priests, perhaps to die in peace. Some of those who still had some health, strength, and willpower went to help those in need. Meanwhile, someone near the door of the little prince's house was shouting for the Priest, the two Bishops, and the Cardinal to come out, as they wanted to speak with them. The Priest responded to the call, and the person told him the message. The Priest then relayed the situation to the two Bishops and the Cardinal, and they quickly said goodbye to the mother, blessing her once more as they left.

They told me that as the Priest, the two Bishops, and the Cardinal were leaving the house, they still looked fatigued, as if they needed sleep, but their faces showed smiles, indicating they were very happy. Upon exiting the door, they took some gourds to drink water from a bucket by the entrance, drinking deeply, as if they had been in a desert for two or three days without water. After quenching their thirst, they wanted to sit down, but the person who had brought the message insisted once more that they go see the people who were dying and asking for their help, perhaps to die in peace.

They told me that they immediately went to the house of the sick, the Priest, the two Bishops, and the Cardinal. Upon seeing them, without even examining them closely, they could see that their skin was swollen, cracked, and dry like fish scales, with a color resembling a mixture of purple, ash, and crushed coal with blood. The skin was also peeling off as if it were melting. Immediately, they did the same as they had done with the little prince: they cleared the room of others and locked themselves in with the sick to perform prayers and cleansing rituals, trying to help the sick escape the curse of the little prince of evil. The curse had caused them terrible pain throughout their bodies since the first day they were afflicted, leaving them bedridden, with no one able to cure them.

They told me that the sick emitted a strong stench, just like the little prince when he was angry or when the demon left his body and soul after he exploded. The smell was unbearable, so the Priest, the two Bishops, and the Cardinal had to cover their noses and mouths to endure it. When they sprinkled holy water on the sick and performed exorcism prayers, the patients writhed like snakes, biting their tongues between their teeth, screaming, and groaning in a strange way that was difficult to understand. The curious onlookers thought they heard the sick people muttering, deliriously saying, "the little prince, the little prince," blaming the little prince for their suffering and the cruel delirium they were experiencing. They were not mistaken—the little prince knew what they were feeling, and he was the only one who was happy about their suffering.

They told me that the Priest, the two Bishops, and the Cardinal spent a long time there, perhaps two or three hours, praying and performing exorcisms. They noticed that the sick gradually calmed down as if they were paralyzed and falling asleep until they stopped talking. Their bulging eyes made them look as if they were dead or asleep, with dark, almost melted skin, resembling wax or paper mummies.

They told me that the Priest, the two Bishops, and the Cardinal continued to speak and pray in different languages, blessing the sick with their hands and crucifixes and bathing them in holy water. They also had to help the sick put their tongues back in their mouths, as their tongues seemed to have grown and no longer fit, or they had bitten them in desperation to ease the pain. It was difficult to help them stop biting their tongues because they had already been cut.

They told me that the Priest, the two Bishops, and the Cardinal looked extremely tired but didn't stop blessing and praying. After a long time, they saw the sick begin to move and try to open their eyes. They also looked less pale, but then the sick began growling like wolves, trying to get up and attack the Priest, the two Bishops, and the Cardinal. However, they managed to control them by showing them the crucifixes and pouring a lot of holy water on them until they calmed down and fell asleep, as if hypnotized, with their eyes still bulging. Even in their sleep, they let out groans like dying wolves.

They told me that when the Priest, the two Bishops, and the Cardinal saw that the sick were finally calm, they stopped blessing and praying. They looked almost without strength, barely able to sit down. After a while, they left the room, looking as if they had just come from a desert, exhausted, sweating, and very thirsty. Trembling with fatigue, they drank water eagerly from some jugs nearby, even splashing their faces and heads. They joked among themselves that they had sweated so much because the battle had been tough, extremely challenging and exhausting, but that they had worked together, united as a team, and managed to defeat the demon, freeing those dying people from the possession that had nearly taken their lives. They had expelled the demon from the souls of those people, who had been possessed and whom the demon had cruelly tried to exterminate, along with the population and their faith.

They told me that after a while, the Priest, the two Bishops, and the Cardinal checked on the sick again and saw that they were no longer melting, that their skin was no longer falling off. They carefully observed them to make sure they were indeed well, and when they confirmed that everything seemed normal compared to how they had been, they said they were fine. They left the room, breathing deeply, as if they couldn't believe it. That's why the Priest, the two Bishops, and the Cardinal were happy, saying they had won another battle against Satan. With joy, they celebrated as if they had won a poker game or their favorite team had scored a goal, raising their hands in triumph. Then, with newfound strength, they celebrated with a delicious cup of coffee brought to them by some kind women. With pride, they almost cried alongside all the people present, overcome with emotion. The Priest, the two Bishops, and the Cardinal said that as a team, no matter how many times Satan stood in their way, they would defeat him. They shouted with joy, saying that God's power was unique, unbeatable, and they would stay united to defeat him wherever he appeared, proudly declaring that if he dared to confront them again, they would be ready to face him.

They told me that once they had rested a bit, they found the strength to joke and, in loud voices so that the people around could hear, they said: "A town united by faith will never be defeated by Satan or anyone else." The people who heard what the Priest, the two Bishops, and the Cardinal said drew strength from their shattered souls, and with joy, they also shouted and waved their hands, holding their faces in disbelief at what they were experiencing after an exterminating nightmare that had claimed the lives of hundreds of people and thousands of wild and domestic animals. Only a few cats, dogs, pigs, chickens, cows, and other animals had managed to survive such a terrible curse, which they shouldn't have been subjected to.

As the day passed and the hours slipped away, the Priest, the two Bishops, and the Cardinal, along with the people who accompanied them, remained excited, recounting the difficult story of the nightmare they had lived through. All with their little cups of coffee in their hands, they appeared to have almost forgotten the suffering they had endured just hours before. The joy of having ended the curse of the little prince and the evil nightmare they had been subjected to seemed, at that moment, to be a distant memory, as if it had happened many years ago.

So happy and content they were, or believed they would be, that all of them—the Priest, the two Bishops, the Cardinal, and the few survivors present—repeated that a town united by faith will never be defeated by Satan or anyone else. They had united their forces to banish him from their town and their souls, which he had begun to possess. The scars left on their bodies, and the memories of those they lost—both family members and beloved animals who were a source of their livelihood—would perhaps stay with them until they died. Thanks to that beautiful baby, that capricious little boy, who was none other than the devil himself who took over his body and soul, they too had paid with their lives.

They told me that the people from whom the Priest, the two Bishops, and the Cardinal had expelled the demon still lay in their beds as if in a deep sleep. Their eyes and tongues still showed signs of injury, but their skin seemed to be returning to its original color. Unfortunately, they remained weakened by the suffering they had endured, unable to eat, drink water, or be healed. No one understood how they survived for so many days without eating or drinking, which led them to believe that God was with these people. However, due to their misfortune or innocence, they had mocked the little prince and were punished with a terrible illness that nearly cost them their lives. But they were grateful, thanking the religious men—the Priest, the two Bishops, and the Cardinal—who arrived just in time to save them, snatching them from the cruel and wicked intentions that the beautiful little prince had subjected them to.

They told me that soon after, the Priest, the two Bishops, and the Cardinal left the house of the sick and returned to the house of the little prince. They asked the mother how the little prince, whom they had rescued from the clutches of the demon, was behaving. The mother, smiling with certainty, replied that he was behaving like any other newborn. She had fed him canned milk from a bottle, and he took it without any problem. He hadn't thrown any tantrums or shown any signs of anger; he hadn't cried and was just sleeping peacefully.

They told me that the Priest, the two Bishops, and the Cardinal entered the room to check on the little prince. They sensed that he no longer smelled like he did when Satan was expelled from his soul. Satisfied with what the mother had told them and what they were seeing, they believed that everything the mother said was true. They blessed him again and began speaking in other languages, and this time, the little prince didn't scream like a boar or fighting rats. They only saw him open and close his eyes, as if the light or daylight was too bright for him.

They told me that everything went as the religious men had hoped. This time, there were no bursts of lightning, demonic winds, devastating earthquakes, torrential rains, or destructive hailstorms. They observed the little prince and saw that he no longer had fiery eyes or a snake-like tongue. He didn't writhe like a snake when they sprinkled holy water on him. The Priest, the two Bishops, and the Cardinal were delighted to see that the little prince even smiled when the holy water touched his body.

They told me that when the religious men were sure they had completed their work with the blessings and the exorcism, they removed the mantle they had covered the little prince with when they laid him next to his mother. They saw that his stomach had healed, that it was no longer bleeding, and that the wound from his explosion had closed up. The religious men laughed, sighed deeply, and whistled with joy, jokingly wiping the sweat from their brows as if to say they were sure they had defeated the demon and that it would never return to the little prince's body.

They told me that the Priest, the two Bishops, and the Cardinal, to be sure they had indeed won the battle against Satan, woke the little prince to perform a new cleansing ritual. They placed several crucifixes around his neck and chest to see how he would react to them. They were so surprised to see the little prince start smiling and playing with them, even putting them in his mouth as if trying to eat them. The mother was just as surprised as the religious men to see her little boy seemingly having fun with the relics placed on his chest. Grateful, the mother got up as best she could and embraced the religious men, repeatedly thanking them for saving her son from such an incredible curse.

They told me that the religious men kindly and proudly replied that she shouldn't worry, as that was their job. They had been sent by God, and they were his soldiers, tasked with defeating Satan whenever and wherever he appeared or hid in someone's body. Their mission was to defeat him before he could destroy someone's faith. But unfortunately, this time, it had been extremely difficult to banish him, to expel him from the souls that survived that horrible suffering. For several days, with great satanic, perverse, and diabolical power, the entire town, which had been happy and peaceful just weeks before, had been subjected to his power. Some hundreds of people couldn't withstand the curse that had fallen upon them and had to pay with their lives, suffering a cruel and undeserved punishment.

They told me that the Priest, the two Bishops, and the Cardinal, surprised but smiling with joy, left the room of the mother and the little prince. This time, they no longer looked like they had come from a desert, tired, sweaty, and thirsty. They were smiling, content with their triumph, their victory over Satan. Finally, they could see some tranquility in the people who continued to suffer from the devastation caused by the little prince of evil. The Priest, the two Bishops, and the Cardinal quietly told each other that they shouldn't let their guard down because Satan is not to be trusted, not even for a moment. But their duty was to help the people feel at ease and to help them heal their wounds, both physical and, more importantly, those in their souls, so they could recover and return to the happiness, peace, and joy that their lives had been just a few days before.

They told me that after leaving the room, despite being so exhausted, they found the energy deep within their souls to keep going, so they no longer seemed tired. They asked the people if they could bless them, and everyone agreed. They began blessing everyone present with holy water and crucifixes. They invited the people to join them in blessing the living, the dead, the severely injured, and the sick in their homes, as well as the few animals they could find—chickens, goats, dogs, donkeys, horses, and other animals that showed themselves. It seemed that the animals, like the survivors, could sense that Satan was no longer among them, and they were happy to fly through the air, run through the muddy, destroyed streets, and be free once more.

They told me that in the pastures and fields, some cows and other animals showed signs of happiness. Wild birds flew through the skies, carried by the fresh air and the beautiful sunlight, which also smiled upon them, illuminating the devastated landscape as it broke through the dark clouds that had hidden it. The once ominous clouds, which had unleashed torrential rains and terrifying tornadoes, had finally disappeared, leaving the sky clear and blue.

They told me that although the people still felt uneasy, they tried to smile and even let out a few laughs. Their dirty and tired faces showed the happiness they had regained, though still with some disbelief. But together with the Priest, the two Bishops, and the Cardinal, they held onto their faith in God. Everyone who could walk and wasn't occupied caring for the dead or tending to the wounded found the strength to support each other. They went out to pray among the ruins of the destroyed streets and to bless the graves where they had buried the people and animals who had lost their lives in the cursed storm brought by the little prince of evil.

They also told me that some relatives of those who hadn't yet been buried asked the religious men to accompany them when they laid their loved ones to rest, as they believed that with their blessings, Satan would not trouble them again, even in their graves. The religious men proudly responded that, of course, they would accompany them, as they had been sent by God to help them in whatever they needed and to ensure that Satan would never return to torment them with his tricks.

They told me that after the funerals, the Priest, the two Bishops, and the Cardinal walked through some of the fields and near the rivers, blessing the animals, who seemed to understand that these religious men were their saviors. The animals approached them as if to thank them for helping them and saving them from being massacred like the thousands who couldn't withstand the severe punishments that the little prince of evil had inflicted upon them. The animals had suffered just as the people had, and they too had once been happy, only to experience the worst punishment of their lives a few days later—a malignant curse that still lingered among them.

They told me that as the Priest, the two Bishops, and the Cardinal went around praying and blessing, dozens of injured animals, some barely able to move, crawled out of their hiding places as if they knew that being blessed would bring them relief. The animals appeared very happy, with some dogs, donkeys, pigs, horses, and cows rolling around in the muddy puddles out of sheer joy as the holy water fell on their bodies. Each animal expressed its happiness in its way— whinnying, barking, or braying. Chickens, goats, and other animals also seemed to sense that it was all over.

They told me that the animals showed their happiness and enjoyed their newfound freedom, no longer feeling the fear of the curse that had plagued them. The chickens clucked, the roosters crowed, the horses, donkeys, goats, and other animals started to run around, and the wild birds were once again seen flying in the skies above that devastated place. The pigs in their pens and other animals were already asking for food. Seeing the animals' happiness, the people also began to laugh with joy, commenting on how the animals seemed to have more willpower than they did. They said that this couldn't be possible, and together they began to seek solutions on how to rebuild their lives, their homes, and start to recover everything they had lost in the demonic destruction caused by the little prince of evil, who had tried to destroy their faith and their lives by hiding in the body and soul of that innocent child, who had not yet been born but had already been conceived in the body of that noble woman.

They told me that they went around praying and blessing all the places, people, and animals in the devastated little town until nightfall. Then, they all gathered in the church, which was the only building that had withstood the storms. They spent a few hours together, sharing their strength and faith, trying to return to their normal lives without feeling the cruelty of the sadness brought on by the suffering they had endured at the hands of that charming little prince of evil. But with the help of God, who had sent his soldiers to fight Satan alongside them, and with their faith, the religious men had defeated him with the power of their prayers.

They told me that when the Priest, the two Bishops, and the Cardinal left the devastated little town, the people stayed behind to continue caring for the sick and watching over them, while also tending to the injured animals. Others focused on burying the newly deceased people and animals who hadn't survived the curse of the little prince of evil. Many of the severely injured continued to suffer, crying out in sadness, anguish, despair, and pain, feeling powerless and uncertain about what they would do with their lives, having lost almost everything.

They told me that although they wanted to maintain faith and willpower to avoid despair, some people were still crying, encouraging each other to recover soon from the terrible nightmare, the ruthless massacre they had suffered. They trusted that God's soldiers had defeated Satan and destroyed him forever, that the curse of the little prince had passed and would never return, that Satan had lost the war and all the battles on this blessed land. They believed he had left their lives, unable to take away their faith in God, and that, as the demon he was, he fled, crying in the rain and the darkness of the night, back to the very hell from which he had come to try to destroy the peace and faith in God in that community.

They told me that the sick who had suffered from the storm or the curse of the little prince gradually began to recover. They looked happy, and after about three days, those who had fallen ill with the death of animals no longer coughed or suffered from fever or chills. Those who had mocked the little prince no longer had their skin melting; their skin was regaining its color, and when they walked or talked, they seemed almost recovered. They no longer felt pain or feared for their lives, although some scars from the past remained on their bodies and in their souls, scars that might never fully heal, but even so, in their convalescence, with little strength in their bodies but strong in their souls, they had faith that they could forget what they had suffered.

They told me that for a time, no one visited the little prince and his mother. It seemed they held a grudge for what they had experienced, even though the Priest, the two Bishops, and the Cardinal had explained before leaving the town that they should not bear any resentment toward them, that they too had been victims of the ruthless, evil deed that Satan had sent upon them so that everyone would suffer the pleasure of his terrifying punishment for being a town of faith, of goodness, and faithful believers in God. But even though they had suffered his merciless punishment, Satan could not defeat them. With their infinite faith, they had managed to send him back to the very hell from which he had emerged.

They told me that the only help the little prince received was from his mother, who was the only one taking care of him. The people were still fearful that what they had suffered in the past days might happen again, even though the Priest, the two Bishops, and the Cardinal had explained that neither the little prince nor his mother was to blame for what had happened. The child was just as much a victim as they were, and Satan was the only culprit who had tried to destroy them because they were a united people with faith in each other and in God. They knew they were a humble town, and all its people were generous, sharing love among themselves.

They told me that it was indeed a very peaceful town where everyone trusted everyone. At all times, people greeted each other, and they had adopted a tradition about fifteen years before the catastrophic curse. Each and every one of the inhabitants would light a candle every day, once in the afternoon and again at night, indicating that everything was fine in their home. Not lighting it meant something was wrong in that family, whether due to illness or a possible tragedy. Dozens of people would gather just to socialize in a small garden or in the churchyard.

During family gatherings, such as baptisms, weddings, or a young girl's quinceañera, the entire town would come together. They would usually gather to have some coffee or play a game of cards or lottery, but it was mainly about simply spending time together and showing that they could trust each other. Everyone would invite one another, socializing without any problems. No one disrespected the women, the elderly, the young girls, or the children who walked alone through the streets without any fear of being humiliated or kidnapped. Everyone looked out for each other, and the older folks would advise the younger ones, whether or not they were their children or siblings. The youth respected the elders as they did their parents and grandparents.

They also had the courtesy and precaution that when a relative of someone living there visited, the person being visited would introduce them to almost the entire community. If someone visited the town, there was always someone to attend to them or introduce them to others so that they would feel comfortable and part of the community, following the social model they had. The entire community was very peaceful and well-organized, with no crime or evil present for more than two decades. That's why they believed God had blessed them.

They told me that perhaps this was the reason for Satan's envy, that he wanted to destroy them. That was why he disguised himself as a beautiful baby, whom everyone called "the little prince," but under the force of the demon, he became the little prince of evil. His fury claimed the lives of some hundreds of humans and thousands of innocent animals, who, through no fault of their own, had to pay with their lives for the proud pleasure of that demon who had escaped from hell to come to earth to rob them of their faith and their lives. But with the faith of all and the help of the religious soldiers that God sent them—the Priest, the two Bishops, and the Cardinal—Satan did not achieve all that he had desired. With his selfishness and anger at not being able to complete his game, he raged, crying like a crow or rabid rats fighting, as he was sent back to the very hell from which he had emerged.

They told me that about two weeks later, the physical wounds of the injured people were almost healed, but more importantly, they felt that their souls were recovering. They felt even more secure in their faith and their health because, in those days, the Priest, the two Bishops, and the Cardinal returned to the town to remind them or make them feel that neither God nor they would abandon them. They promised to continue visiting to ensure that Satan would not try to return and disrupt their faith or their lives or attempt to finish them off with another terrible, diabolical trick or a new one of his games.

They told me that they called the people to speak with them in the small town church. Almost everyone gathered, except for some who truly couldn't walk, were very sick, or were busy. The little prince and his mother were also absent. Perhaps the mother didn't want to go, as she knew very well that the people still held resentment toward her since no one visited or spoke to her. She preferred to stay at home, alone with her son, to avoid feeling rejected or insulted by anyone. No one had even gone to inform them, as they still harbored some fear of them. No one wanted to hear or know anything about them, fearing that something diabolical might happen to them if they got too close. That's why no one went near their house, much less spoke to or visited them. It was too soon for them to have forgotten the suffering and resentment they had lived through, which had entered their souls. Even though they tried not to hate them, they couldn't resist, as they still bore the scars on their bodies and souls that hadn't healed, making it hard for them to forgive and forget what they had suffered.

They told me that when the Priest noticed that the little prince and his mother were not present, he asked someone to go get them and invite them to come. Everyone protested at the same time, saying they didn't want them there. Despite having been explained that they too were victims of Satan's evil, they didn't want to understand. They felt hatred or mistrust at the thought of seeing them, which is why they refused to obey. They didn't want anyone to go invite them or let anyone fetch them. The Priest, the two Bishops, and the Cardinal pleaded with them, asking them to please go and bring them, but no one obeyed.

They told me that the people, outraged, ignored the pleas of the Priest, the two Bishops, and the Cardinal. The pleas only agitated them, and they began to insult and curse the little prince and his mother, blaming them for their destruction, for the evil they had suffered. Their hatred was so strong that they forgot they were inside a church, a place they should have respected, as well as the holy religious figures who had come to visit them. Seeing the little prince and his mother among them would have been difficult; having them nearby could have led to a mistake, such as hitting or insulting them inside the church. That's why they refused to obey the pleas of those who had restored peace to their lives and souls. The townspeople were unwilling to understand these reasons, as they said their wounds were still bleeding too much to consider forgiving them, even though they perhaps refused to accept that both the mother and the baby had also been used by Satan, as the religious figures had already explained.

They told me that the Priest, the two Bishops, and the Cardinal asked for forgiveness on behalf of the little prince and his mother, but the people wouldn't accept it, insisting on blaming them for the curse. When they saw the people's refusal, the Priest and a Bishop attempted to go get them, but the people, very agitated, forcibly stopped them, standing in their way and blocking their path. The people continued to insist that they didn't want to see them there, saying that if they came, they would leave because no one wanted to see them. They refused to accept them among them, feeling too hurt by their past suffering to forget and accept them into their lives as if nothing had happened. To the townspeople, the scars on their bodies and souls still seemed to be bleeding, which is why they refused to follow the orders of the religious figures and see among them those they considered responsible for the misfortune that had occurred to them, as if they could forget it overnight.

They told me that the Priest, the two Bishops, and the Cardinal spent some time trying to convince the people, but it seemed impossible. It took nearly half an hour of the religious figures' pleading and urging before the people finally calmed down and agreed to let them go and bring the mother and the little prince. But no one wanted to go fetch them, so the Priest and a Bishop went to invite them to come to the church. Although all the people were unhappy, no one had left, criticizing and murmuring, as if eager with anger, watching where they might come from, perhaps wishing to insult them or demand that they leave, that no one wanted them in that place, that they were despised.

They told me that when the Priest and the Bishop arrived at the church with the little prince and his mother, the people looked at them with anger and mistrust but said nothing. Some seemed like they wanted to leave, others murmured, and they were so upset that it seemed they wanted to lynch them. Some people, perhaps those who had lost family members, left because they couldn't bear the presence of those they considered responsible for their families' deaths in the terrible massacre caused by the curse of the little prince of evil.

They told me that some people remained upset at seeing the little prince, who had brought about their suffering. They prayed and thanked God for delivering them from such a terrible misfortune. Some people even wanted to leave because they couldn't bear the presence of the little prince and his mother. That's why the Priest, the two Bishops, and the Cardinal, seeing how angry they were, began to explain what is said in the prayers: "Forgive us our trespasses, as we forgive those who trespass against us," and that if they didn't forgive, they were becoming servants of Satan. They said that they would be worse than the little prince because the little prince was just a victim; Satan had only used that baby as a shield to reach them, to try to destroy them. But they were acting with the intention of evil, knowing that they were hating an innocent child who had not asked for Satan to be conceived in his body. That baby was innocent of all guilt, just as they and everyone who had died, and the entire community, were. All had been victims of Satan, the religious figures said, and we were witnesses, and many of you saw it too.

They told me that the Priest, the two Bishops, and the Cardinal invited the people to reflect, insisting that they had demonstrated that they were a people of faith, a people of God, and that in their pure souls, they should not harbor hatred or resentment. They reminded them that God forgave those who crucified Him, so why couldn't they forgive the little prince, who, like them, was merely another victim of Satan? They explained that the little prince, even from his mother's womb, had suffered the curse of being Satan's instrument. The Priest, the two Bishops, and the Cardinal pleaded once more, asking them to understand and reflect on the possibility that the little prince might suffer this curse throughout his life. They urged them to forgive and to promise never to hate again, to see the little prince and his mother as they would any other child and mother. Only then could their souls find happiness, for hatred would only destroy them from within, preventing them from being as they were before Satan's curse.

With these strong and precise words, the townspeople, not entirely convinced, rubbed their faces and scratched their heads, searching within themselves for the response they could give. Could they accept the faith of forgiveness, or would their conscience lead them to believe that they were siding with Satan, as the religious figures suggested? It was then that some began to reflect, expressing to others that the religious figures were right in what they were saying and doing. Gradually, people, through sighs and sobs, asked the religious figures for forgiveness, to which they replied that the forgiveness should be directed to the mother and the child, as they were the ones who truly needed it, for they were not to blame for the tragedy that had befallen them.

They told me that because of these words, so clear and true, they were able to forgive. With a hug given to the religious figures, the mother, and the child, they sobbed with joy, feeling that their souls had been relieved of the burden of resentment that had been destroying them. It had been a heavy cross they carried in their souls, one that would have been very difficult to bear for the rest of their lives. The hatred had been eating away at their hearts, preventing them from living in peace. Thanks to the blessed words of the religious figures, they asked for forgiveness, and the mother, holding the little prince in her arms, granted it. The mother said she understood them, explaining that she had never harbored any resentment toward them because she and her son had also felt the pain caused by Satan. As a mother, seeing her child suffer under that curse and being unable to help him was a terrible and macabre torment for her. She thanked them repeatedly on behalf of herself and her son for their understanding.

They told me that when the Priest, the two Bishops, and the Cardinal blessed the people, they first did so with the little prince and the mother to see how he would react when holy water was sprinkled on him. The little prince was asleep, and everyone was amazed because he didn't even move, as if he felt nothing. Some noticed that he even opened his eyes slightly, made a gesture, and smiled. Seeing this, the people, now filled with regret for the harm they had done through their disdain and rejection, no longer felt content.

They told me that some people cried, while others only sobbed, asking for forgiveness from the mother and the religious figures. They felt their bodies breaking, as if their souls were almost escaping due to the immense suffering they had endured. The relief that their souls experienced, now free of the hatred they had harbored within, made them feel very happy. Many even wept because they no longer held any resentment toward the little prince. The entire community, with the love among them and their faith in God, had remained intact, and Satan had finally lost his war against them. Through their shared faith, they had defeated him.

They told me that when the Priest, the two Bishops, and the Cardinal were leading the prayers and giving blessings, there were no longer any bursts of destructive winds or terrifying lightning. The torrential rains and marble-sized hailstones were no longer present. Everything was as it had been months earlier. The sun illuminated the destroyed village, which, though already receiving aid for reconstruction, remained almost as devastated as before. The lovely baby, whom they could now call the little prince, did not cry like fighting rats or a trapped boar when the holy water touched his body. His eyes did not turn fiery red, nor did he stick out his tongue like a snake.

They told me that everyone was amazed and surprised, feeling assured that God was now with them, protecting them from all evil. They trusted that God would never abandon them again and that their faith would continue with them for the rest of their lives. They could finally be at peace, even though they still felt the pain and sadness of losing family members to the little prince's evil and also the loss of many of their animals, homes, and belongings. But with God's help, they could remember it as if it were a dream or a nightmare that was difficult to forget.

They told me that the little prince had honey-colored eyes and a normal tongue like any other child. The child was, as they said, "as beautiful as a little prince, the child everyone talked about from the very first second of his life!" The child everyone believed would bring happiness to that place, but just hours after his birth, after arriving in this world, to the earth he desired to destroy, they began to feel the fury of his evil and his pleasure in watching them suffer. Some witnessed him as he slowly murmured, uttering his last words, asking God to take him away, imposing on them the ruthless curse that, for just over three weeks, destroyed their happiness, their homes, and their peace, cowardly taking the lives of some, along with hundreds of animals that also paid with their lives for the terrible curse of Satan, who had transformed into the little prince of evil, descending to earth only to mock the faith and goodness of those people whose only sin was having the faith they shared among themselves, a faith they professed daily like breakfast, which the demon, with his envy and power, sought to destroy with cruel malice.

They told me that the people had calmed down, listening only to the prayers and blessings given by the Priest, the two Bishops, and the Cardinal. Some began to smile and socialize with others. When the meeting ended, the Priest, the two Bishops, and the Cardinal decided to go out and bless those who couldn't attend due to their health, as they were still badly injured. They invited those present who could walk to accompany them, as some still had not fully recovered, their wounds from the body not yet healed, the malevolent, ruthless tortures they had suffered too deep and terrible, leaving some struggling to walk or barely able to rise from where they were seated or lying.

They also told me that for a few hours, they walked and blessed the devastated streets, the few and destroyed houses that had withstood the evil of the little prince. They also visited the graves of all the deceased and the places used as cemeteries to bury the hundreds of animals that also lost their lives due to the ruthless fury of the little prince of evil, who, after mocking them, mercilessly massacred them.

They told me that it was the little prince's mother who asked the Priest, the two Bishops, and the Cardinal how they knew that her son had been the messenger of Satan, sent to destroy the faith of that community and take the lives of some people and the hundreds of animals that also died because of her son's wickedness. The Priest answered that he had a dream in which a tall, slender woman in a white dress, slightly disheveled, came to his door and told him what was happening in this community. She asked him to please come to their aid, saying that this town needed him. She didn't say exactly what they needed, only that they urgently needed his help. When he woke up, he realized it was just a dream, as he was still lying down with no woman by his side, but he thought to himself, "This is not just a dream; it must be true," and he said to himself, "This must be a message from God!" He knew that a few days earlier, they had been suffering from the disastrous rains, and without a second thought, he came to see what was happening.

They told me that the Priest arrived on horseback because he had left his car in the nearest town to this community. They had told him that his car couldn't enter due to the roads being destroyed, so someone from that town lent him the horse he used to appear for the first time in that devastated community.

They said that the Priest mentioned he never hesitated to come and try to help them, believing that at the very least, he could offer them courage to continue with their lives and their faith. As the Priest shared his dream with them, some began to murmur or comment that there was no doubt that it was God who had sent that woman to save them because she was exactly as the Priest described her, just like the woman they had all seen arriving in the town a few days after they had been suffering from the curse that the little prince, in his fury, terror, and death, had unleashed upon them without mercy or compassion, with the worst cruelty he could inflict. The wounds still bled less painfully, but they were still deeply affected, with immense sadness and pain seared into their souls.

They told me that the woman who had discovered the little prince of evil was never heard from again, never returning to that town. Hundreds of people who visited the place said that no one knew her or had ever heard of her before. That's why the Priest, the two Bishops, the Cardinal, and those who survived the disastrous evil of the little prince were all certain that the tall, slender woman was indeed God or a celestial angel sent by Him. The Priest, the two Bishops, and the Cardinal were merely His faithful servants, the soldiers who carried out His orders, which were to defeat the demon that had taken over the body of that small baby and to restore health, love, tranquility, peace, and faith to all those who had survived the terrible massacre of the little prince of evil so that they would no longer have to endure his disastrous wickedness, for whenever he threw his tantrums, the torturous punishment and ruthless massacre began for every living being in that town.

They told me that everyone believed that it truly was God, but in the form of that woman, or that it was indeed a celestial angel sent by Him, who returned to heaven to continue watching over and blessing all those who survived the massacre that the little prince of evil unleashed upon them without mercy or compassion. They believed that from the divine infinite, by God the Father's command, this celestial being would watch over humanity and all living beings on this blessed earth, protecting them from any other mischief, ruthless prank, or evil deed that Satan might want to unleash upon them.

They told me that after the Priest, the two Bishops, and the Cardinal finished blessing everyone and everything that survived the ruthless massacres unleashed by the little prince of evil on their town and their faith, the people talked about the tragedy as if it were a story they had heard, a nightmare from a bad dream. However, they still carried it deep within their souls and had it etched into their skin—a tragic reality they had suffered, felt, and lived through, one that few could escape. It was a devastating nightmare, and at least they wanted to believe that it was just a story or a horrible nightmare that all the survivors, along with the animals, experienced during a bad night. It wasn't simply a cruel twist of fate trying to destroy them completely, wiping out everything that had life there. Tens of people and animals still bore the damage on their bodies from such terrible evil.

They told me that a short time later, a couple of hours after the blessings, the people gathered in the church. They all cooperated and made a meal with the little they had left to thank and bid farewell to the Priest, the two Bishops, and the Cardinal, who served as God's soldiers, warriors in battle, to defeat Satan himself, who had disguised himself as a prince, descending from hell to try to destroy their lives and faith. But God was always with them, and despite all the fury and demonic pleasure Satan unleashed against them, their faith was never defeated.

They told me something incredible and humane—a true act of charity, admiration, and respect for the surviving animals of that devastating massacre, something that fills all the survivors with pride. All the visitors who know about the tragedy admire and respect them with great pride because, despite their hunger and need for food, they did not kill any of the surviving animals for consumption. On the contrary, they considered them sacred. The entire surviving population promised to protect and care for them as a blessing or a memory until their lives ended naturally. This is why the thousands of visitors who come to the community admire and respect them when they hear this story.

They told me that the Priest, the two Bishops, and the Cardinal left the destroyed town, and the people who had left the town, those who had managed to escape out of fear of the little prince of evil's curse, returned to try to rebuild their lives and homes. Many others who no longer lived there or worked outside the town also returned to join those who had endured the terrible massacre of the little prince of evil. Together, they gathered at the place where they first saw the Lady of God, the celestial angel sent by Him. It was there that they all prayed and gave thanks to the one they called the Lady of God, who came from heaven to protect, bless, and care for them from the very demon who had massacred them for so long. But God came to their aid, and with His infinite divine power, He defeated Satan and sent him back to the hell from which he came.

It is known that in the very place where the Lady of God appeared, the townspeople, along with others from nearby communities, promised to make a pilgrimage, praying from the church to the spot where the Lady of God first appeared. They believe that with these prayers, their souls and town will remain protected by God's blessing so that Satan will not dare to return and attempt another of his evil tricks.

They told me that some visitors asked them why they named the small church they built where she first appeared "Lady of God." The townspeople explained that they all agreed to name it that because the angel who first came to help them appeared in the form of a woman, and to honor God in her name, they decided to call it the "Lady of God."

It is known that among the people of that community and others, they created a beautiful garden with a small church in the center, where there is a statue of the Lady of God. They commissioned a local sculptor to create the statue to place it in that spot as a symbol of their faith. The community promised to hold an annual celebration in honor of the Lady of God, inviting other communities to participate.

As with everything in life, time passed—the days, weeks, months, and years have gone by since that community of God suffered the fateful, malevolent massacre, the evil, indiscriminate tragedy that Satan, in the form of a beautiful baby, whom everyone called the little prince at birth, unleashed upon them just a few days after his birth. They continued to call him the little prince but of evil because they believed he was the cause of the worst tragedy known in the history of their town or any other nation on the planet.

It is known that to honor and remember the Lady of God, the beautiful garden that the community and others from nearby towns maintain is named "The Lady of God." This makes them feel happy about their faith and their town. They say they feel like they are messengers of God because hundreds of people who hear them talk about their tragedy consider them a living example to follow. These people have regained their lost faith in God and in everything they want to do, living their lives with enthusiasm and joy. This is why when visitors come to the garden where the small church with the statue of the Lady of God is located, they all pray and praise, asking for God's blessing for health and for never losing faith in His divine goodness.

It is known that the townspeople and people from other villages asked the Priest who first came to their aid to stay and tend to the two small churches as a symbol of respect and honor for the blessing they received from God. They believed that having the Priest, who was one of the soldiers who defeated the demon, as a historian during his masses would make visiting worshippers feel more inspired in their faith and beliefs, seeing him as an example to follow. This is why he has lived in that community for some time now, chosen as a faithful messenger of

God, ensuring that Satan will not dare to return and attempt another one of his tricks.

They told me that they continue the tradition of the pilgrimage from the church they already had to the other small church built in the garden where the statue of the Lady of God is located. Every year, they hold religious festivities in her memory, with several mariachi bands and musical groups coming to sing songs or recite poems. Many singers, poets, writers, and mariachis have composed songs and verses for the Lady of God and the soldiers who defeated Satan in that difficult battle. The same Priest, the two Bishops, and the Cardinal, who were God's soldiers and who, with the strength that God gave them through their faith, managed to defeat the demon who had taken over the body and soul of that beautiful baby, come to officiate the masses.

They told me that the state government, in collaboration with the municipal and federal governments, declared the town to be in complete destruction. The governor of the state, under orders from the president of the republic, was required to personally visit the town to see how they could help. When he arrived and saw the town completely destroyed, the governor called the president and told him what had happened. Images of the destruction were sent to him via satellite. Immediately upon seeing the images, the president ordered assistance to be sent. This is why, the day after the governor arrived, construction materials, machinery, and some architects were sent to rebuild the houses of all those in that suffering town.

They told me that the people who survived the malevolent tragedy were very moved when the government and people from other towns provided help. It was a very welcome aid, and the townspeople, in every mass and celebration, give thanks to everyone who helped them. At the entrances and exits of the town, they placed large plaques and signs engraved with their gratitude for the valuable assistance.

They told me, and I also witnessed during my visit, that they opened a free clinic for the injured to continue recovering. They also provided financial aid for people to buy personal items like clothes, furniture, and beds, to replace what they had lost. They were given tractors, fertilizers, and pesticides to cultivate their lands and dozens of cows and bulls to form a cooperative to increase their livestock. Many people from other towns brought hundreds of other animals as gifts, including chickens, turkeys, goats, and sheep, to help change their lives and help them forget the nightmare they had lived through.

They told me they believe that almost the entire world knows about their tragedy and their beliefs because they have seen dozens of tourists from faraway nations arrive. These tourists might feel curiosity or a desire to see and experience the memory that the people share whenever they are asked. They notice that these visitors leave feeling very different, excited, and with a joy they had never experienced before. Many write down what they ask and what they are told, while others record the questions and answers on their cell phones and video cameras.

All the survivors make an effort not to remember the evil nightmare, the twisted pleasure that Satan took in mocking them for a few weeks. Through his cruel and ruthless trick, disguised as a beautiful baby, he descended from hell to destroy their faith and their lives. He mocked not only the people but nearly wiped out all life in that place. However, many still bear indelible marks on their bodies, and all carry them in their souls. But with their faith in God, who helped them, they have managed not to suffer when recalling the terrible curse of that demon, who was once a little prince but a prince of evil. Now that Satan has fled from his body and soul, both the little prince and his mother visit the small churches and walk the same streets where the unforgettable evil tragedy occurred, which they have named: THE TRAGEDY OF THE LITTLE PRINCE OF EVIL.

FLOWERS FROM THE FIELD SHE GATHERED

Flowers from the field she gathered is a story as sad as it is cruel, and it is very different from all others written by well-known writers or novelists who lived in times when almost every human being believed in superstitions, satanic beliefs, witchcraft, and other perverse rituals of the devil.

This story I write today is with the desire to reach all hearts and stay within those who are kind enough to read it or have a great taste for reading, as many people use reading as medicine for stress and relaxation to stop thinking about unpleasant things when they feel frustrated by life's problems.

The story is about a young girl who, from the tender age of five until her mysterious disappearance, was the victim of infamous accusations, cowardly attacked, despised, and humiliated by superstitious people in some of the communities where she lived.

No one knows how the little girl possessed a divine spirit of the old woman who cared for her and protected her from the deranged perverts who wanted to ruin her life. All those people received a cruel punishment as perverse as what they wanted to do, finding a cruel death at the moment they tried to commit their misdeeds. For the townspeople, it was cruel and inhumane, something they did not deserve. Over time, the hatred toward her grew until she left the earth in a very mysterious way that no one knows how it happened.

This is a story that, as I told you, if we were one hundred and twenty years before this twenty-first century, we could say it was real, that everything said in it was true and that, like this tragedy, too many happened because a hundred and twenty years before this century, they did happen. Today, very few people believe in this, but it seems real, as if it really happened in this century. But it is just a pleasant story, which I wholeheartedly hope will interest you. My idea was to make it as believable as possible, so I wrote it as if it had just happened in this twenty-first century, to a young girl barely twenty-five years old. Unfortunately, for that young girl, her birth was cursed. From birth, her fate was marked, a destiny that would be very difficult to live and endure because, from the first breath she took, her suffering began. At the tender age of five, her curse began: her martyrdom, her cruel torture, and her pain, which left her alone in life. She was protected by a celestial soul, the spirit of an old woman who cared for her from birth, rescuing her from the cruel perverted abuses that evil people wanted to subject her to, to satisfy their diabolical instincts of perversity, resulting in an unpleasant tragedy for the people who wanted to commit evil. But since the villagers could not subject her to their perverse illusions and macabre desires, they accused her of being the devil himself or of having a pact with him. The villagers, who still lived, believed that she came to this earth only to suffer, as considered by hundreds of people who knew her, who, with hatred and resentment, cursed her from a very young age as she grew up. Those cruel, perverse, and demonic people commented about her.

Since she was a child, that young girl was cowardly attacked, humiliated with great malice, despised, criticized, and told everything their perverted minds could think of and every word that could come out of their dirty mouths, by cowardly people who, like wild wolves, united to hunt prey. Cruel, perverse people, who, for the simple fact of being an orphan with no one to care for her, support her to guide her life and destiny, no one gave her advice, no one taught her how to solve difficult problems that arose. Just to humiliate her, everyone united.

Since the death of the old woman who came to the community with her, only a young man and a woman everyone considered the ranch's crazy person were occasionally her only company, worrying about her and visiting her from time to time. She never had a friendly hand to protect her, help her not fall, not break in difficult times, let alone when she was very sick, to have a friendly hand that could offer her a glass of water. She never had anyone who loved her a little or at least did not abuse or humiliate her. They always spoke of her with hatred, looked at her with contempt, mocked her, even how she walked, ate, and dressed. Everyone who knew her seemed to unite in groups to attack her, harm her, and no one felt she was worthy of any compassion.

It is believed that those people hated her so much that dozens of them united to try to kill her. Instead, they wanted to lynch her, disappear her from this earth. Because in her youth, she was protected by a super-divine, supernatural power, it seemed that a celestial angel protected her from all the evil planned against her, from all the most macabre atrocities that some perverted psychopaths wanted to do to her, so many of those failed evils ended in disaster for their offenders. That is why the villagers believed she was the devil himself or that she had a pact with him, that she had to be sacrificed to death, tortured, massacred. Many commented that they should burn her alive, that it was the least she deserved.

The fear of hatred they had for her was so great that one day, what they all wished for came true, what they all did to her, the cruelty they prepared for her, the ruthless torture they gave her, the life they condemned her to, which one day hundreds of united murderers wanted to take from her, but they did not succeed. Yet in a very mysterious way, she disappeared from this earth, from the sight of all those cowards who hated her without any consideration or reason, only because of their stupid beliefs.

Perhaps it is like a legend or a myth; you can call it what you want since no one in the communities where she grew up can truly explain what happened, as very few people dare to comment on what happened. They possibly feel remorse for the evil they did and fear that her soul will come from wherever it is to take revenge, as in life, she could not defend herself from the evil they caused her, the ruthless tortures she was subjected to, like a frightened rabbit when an eagle or snake wants to swallow it, and its only salvation is to run and hide.

Just as there are hundreds of legends, stories that people tell, many of which have happened in real life, in a city, on a ranch, on rural roads and alleys, where a person was cowardly massacred or committed suicide, and they believe their souls are wandering because they do not have complete rest or peace they need in their other life.

Such stories or legends talk about all the misfortunes on the planet. Some of these have also been said to occur in towns destroyed by war, bombings with high-powered explosives that destroy everything in their reach, natural disasters, hurricanes, earthquakes, in any country in the world. From them, some great writers or film or novel producers make them known through their stories, gathering relevant information from survivors who tell them how the tragedies happened and how they are leading the pain suffered from such a terrible nightmare they lived.

But as I told you before, today, this story was none of that, it is very different from all those that have been talked about, that you have heard dozens of times, have been told to you, or you have read in a book or newspaper. Everyone who knows this, who lived through those days, is sure that they lived with this reality, and they all talk to each other about how they lived it, now, after what happened, how they reconcile the nightmare they created.

I am going to begin the story of the chilling and cruel story caused by evil people. It is a story that happened to that young girl almost from her first day on earth, one scorching afternoon when the young girl we will discuss today, at just five years old, arrived at those communities for her misfortune, accompanied by an old woman.

No one knows where they came from, nor why she was accompanied by a very old lady who never told anyone the truth when she arrived at that ranch and, near the ranch, in an abandoned house, she stayed to live there. For exactly twenty long, hot, and dusty years, she lived in that abandoned house.

She was just a little pretty girl, possibly just five years old, no one really knows, but according to what the old woman said a few days after arriving at the ranch, due to the immense heat in that region, she died of dehydration. To other people who saw her leave when she ceased to exist, giving her last breath of life, they asked them to take care of the pretty girl, believing they were kind-hearted people.

She stayed for a few days in a house as a guest, but feeling despised and humiliated, realizing there was no place for her in that family, no love or compassion she needed, in her survival instinct, in her little soul, she decided she wanted to be free as the wind, to feel like flying, like a dove in the fresh morning breezes and very hot afternoons, being free to run through the forests, walk by the rivers, climb trees, play with mud and dirt, despite being so young. She seemed to realize that she would live confined, live a punishment she did not deserve. That is why she stayed nowhere; the people in charge of her did not want to have her, saying she was rebellious and did not understand them, that they did not want to be responsible for her, to take care of her. That is why no one really worried about that pretty little girl. That is why she alone adapted to her cruel life, her cruel destiny, alone as a little squirrel or wild kitten to her cruel life, her curse.

Alone, with stones and sticks, she protected herself from the evil people who wanted to do her harm. Since no one cared for her, no one wanted to give her a warm home. Her refuge was the old abandoned house where she arrived with the old woman outside the ranch. Most of her life, she was alone, with no one to pity her, no one visited her; alone, she played, slept, and stayed there.

She talked to no one because she didn't really speak, using signs or murmurs when she asked for help or something to eat, communicating with her little hands and mumbling. Because of that, people and children mocked her when she tried to say or ask for something. Likewise, they laughed at her; not only the children laughed at her, but also the adults mocked her. To further ridicule her, they talked and walked like she did, as she, to make matters worse, had a lame foot, which she dragged a little. It seemed that humiliating her was their daily sustenance. They criticized her appearance, how she dressed, ate, and combed her hair. For everyone, humiliating her and despising her was perhaps more pleasant than having coffee in the morning or having a soda with a piece of bread in the square. For both children, women, and men, she was the entertainment when they saw her. Their perversity was so great that among them all, men, women, and children alike, they tossed her around like an object, cruelly beat her, mocked, and humiliated her.

For many years of her life, she received perverse and humiliating insults since she was left alone after the old woman died, with no one to accompany her. Since she was a little girl, she grew alone from a pretty girl to a beautiful young lady, an adolescent, becoming a beautiful young woman. She almost never combed her hair, never changed her dress, because she only had one, which she had found in the trash a long time ago, and it was the reason some people insulted her, others even cursed her with whatever could come out of their mouths.

Perhaps she did not want to be elegant because she felt happy in her world, she was cheerful, free as the wind, that's how she wanted it, and that's how she decided to live her life. Maybe she didn't have money to buy a comb, luxurious clothes, fashionable clothes, and none of the cowards who criticized her gave them to her or offered her a job to earn them because having her close bothered them. For many who looked at her with contempt, which she did not deserve, they insulted her with great malice and evil.

It was a hot afternoon when the old woman who protected her fell ill from severe dehydration, and to that girl's wicked suffering, that old woman died. For that pretty girl, her innocent life as an orphan was difficult, undesirable, and miserable, not because she asked for it or got it, but because the pain of her sadness and suffering, the cruelty she received, was given by ruthless, perverse people. Maybe that is why, to be a little happy, day after day, she bathed in the rivers and canals and walked through the flowered fields, picking field flowers.

Alone, without anyone's company, like a forgotten puppy or a wild rabbit, she wandered through the fields, along the riverbank, through the sunny, dirty, and dusty streets, that little girl wandered. Nobody cared about anything, dirty, unkempt, in the same little dress, starving, collecting waste from the trash, or what people gave her to humiliate her, some things they threw on the ground for her to pick up and, like the hungry person she was, she devoured them when she ate them, and she was seen like that almost all the time.

She was left alone in this life and lived alone, she seemed to be happy alone because she was seen alone because in the canals, puddles of water, and rivers, she bathed alone, or just to play with the water, she had fun. It was several kilometers of alleys and roads that, jumping and murmuring, singing, happy, smiling sometimes barefoot and with tremendous heat, the little girl traveled, but in the folds of her little dress, to take to the abandoned grave of that old woman, she picked flowers from the field.

Several times she got sick, for hundreds of days, she tasted no food, almost everyone criticized her, judged her, humiliated her, condemned her to a cruel and miserable life, but no one ever showed her the slightest compassion because no one helped her. She solved her problems alone because absolutely no one cared about that pretty little girl.

Even as a little girl, when she picked wildflowers, four ruthless, cowardly, and perverse psychopaths mocked her, trying to take off her clothes. Perhaps their perverse imagination made them think otherwise, maybe to satisfy their malevolent instincts with her body. They amused themselves morbidly with her, even though they saw the little girl terrified by how they treated her. They mocked her even more and groped her body, but those disgusting men never imagined that divine justice, perhaps from the sky or high up on a mountain, would punish them. A coyote that lived in those fields wandered by that day, as if knowing what it was doing. Like a wild animal, fierce like a beast, it defended the pretty and defenseless little girl with teeth and claws as if it were defending its offspring. Those evil, cowardly men, just as they were cowardly, met their deserved fate from that brave coyote.

The fear was too great for those wicked men that even though some tried to escape running out of fear, it was of no use. That brave and ferocious animal caught them in their flight, and they received death mercilessly from that animal. The coyote, the wild animal, having taken its revenge, returned to the little girl, who was still terrified by the fright those perverts caused her. It returned, as if saying goodbye, as if saying, "Don't worry, I am here to defend you!" It caressed her face with its tongue and slid its body against her legs. Once again, crying from fright and adjusting her dress, that little girl was left alone in the field, shedding tears over that cowardly attack, crying her sadness in the field.

Due to what happened to the depraved psychopaths, dozens of men went hunting for that mysterious animal when they found the four perverse cowards dead and torn apart. With dogs and powerful weapons, they hunted it for weeks. Although they heard it howling through the valleys, mountains, rivers, and canals by night or day, no matter how much they searched, they never found it. Tired, they gave up, stopped searching, and, as no one saw what happened, they never blamed the pretty little girl for the men's death. Since then, some people accused her of having a pact with the devil, and out of fear that it might be true, they did not bother her for a long time.

As all little girls do, she grew, and over time she became more beautiful, more lovely. Her body was perfect—her waist, her hips, her breasts, and her height. For many young women in those ranches, their envy of her beauty was very visible on their faces when they saw her. You could notice the envy they had for her. The cowards who looked at her talked about her morbidly. Perhaps the beauty of that young girl bothered them, which is why they liked her even less. But what those perverse people did not understand was that she never asked to be a woman, and her beauty was causing her problems. That's why she was desired by some deranged people, hated and mistreated by young women who envied her. Her beauty was natural; she didn't need to use expensive makeup or perfumes to feel like a woman. She didn't wear expensive clothes, shoes, or luxury necklaces; she didn't need anything to be how she was. Nature had given it to her, the shoes, and the torn dress she wore were found in a dumpster. But because the young girl was beautiful, all the single, married, widowed, or divorced women in nearby ranches were jealous of her, and as always in all the gossip, she was accused by women of being shameless or promiscuous. They accused her of having an easy life with men, single and married, for a few coins or just for being perverted, indulging her crazed lust with any man.

None of what they accused her of was true, because even though she had no one to protect her, she very well knew how to handle the slanders she was accused of and how to get out of them, because there was no evidence against her. There were rumors, but nothing could be proven. She continued alone, had no one in her life, and nobody cared about her. That's why she was always alone, and that's why she was found daily in the clean and crystalline waters of the rivers, where the beauty of her body was reflected when she bathed in its clear waters.

She was a pretty girl and still almost was, having changed a little, becoming a beautiful young woman, and her body was changing. She was as lovely as the butterflies and as beautiful as the wildflowers she picked. That's why some men desired her, and some women hated her. Perhaps she knew nothing of men because she did not desire or want them. She was happy in her solitude, for she was born alone, left alone in life, and did not share her sufferings, sorrows, and pains with anyone. She healed her wounds alone when she hurt or fell. She came to this world alone, and her sufferings, sadness, and misfortunes were lived alone.

The little girl she once was transformed into a beautiful young woman in just a few years. Alone with her problems, sadness, and joys, she faced life's paths with the innocence of youth and her bravery. Whether easy or difficult, she solved them. It seems that to no person did the poor pretty young girl matter at all, for only the field flowers knew of her sadness or her joy. That was her life, and the days passed that way, many months and some years. But that young girl who was despised faced all who mocked her with humility, and a smile was always seen on her face. She didn't care if they humiliated her when they gave her food scraps or when some evil men and women threw them at her face or dress. As cowards always did, like a pack of killer wolves, they mocked her.

Life was never easy for that young girl because wherever someone saw her, the defenseless young girl suffered from insults or abuse. That's why one night, someone tried to take her by force while she slept in her abandoned house. But no one knew what happened. It is believed that the mysterious animal, the same coyote, appeared again, and once again defended the beautiful young girl from being violated, perhaps murdered, like the wild beast it was, defending the defenseless young girl. That cowardly murderer, seeing the animal attacking him, forgot to abuse the beautiful young girl, running scared like an animal. Maybe he didn't realize he was in a pasture, with a fence he rebounded from, and with the barbed wire, that coward, scared, ended up with enormous cuts on his neck and face. Like snake skin, he remained impaled, strangled, well dead. That was the price of his cowardice, paid with his life.

All this seems like a legend because nobody knows the true reality. Maybe the young girl never told it, possibly out of fear that they wouldn't believe her, that they would accuse her of the death. Perhaps it was difficult for her to explain it, because she never commented on it to anyone. No one talked about what she saw, but it was known that they had to bury that coward in a hole in the cemetery.

Her youth was cruel for that beautiful young girl because the tortures and humiliations from all the villagers of that community and nearby ones never stopped. With insults or blows, they always treated her with malicious laughter, mocking her as much as possible. Some men cynically groped her intimate parts, and like madmen celebrated their cynicism as if it were a game of dominoes. But they never realized that divine justice, just like them, with the same cowardice, would charge them for their sin. Because at night, they suffered from an illness that paralyzed their entire body, their skin seemed as if cooked in oil, melting away, purple spots like tumors appeared on parts of their body, bursting and bleeding. With their delicate skin, they could not heal them, and over time, unable to eat or drink anything, not too many days passed when with their life, just like other cowards, with a slow agony, terrible pain, and suffering, they paid for their cowardly actions with their life.

Panic seized the men and some women, too, as they said she might have powers, a divine power, or that perhaps Satan protected her, helped her escape from their perversions, and the ruthless tortures they wanted to subject her to. But the truth was, everyone feared her. All those who treated her with resentment avoided her whenever they saw her passing through the streets. Many did not want to know anything about her because even speaking of her, as they still hated her, they felt as if ice or fire passed through their veins, fear taking hold of them. Just remembering her terrified them. That's why some men and women ran like frightened snakes, as a popular saying in Mexico goes: "fear doesn't ride a donkey," but these villagers feared her as if she was flying an airplane. That's why every time she came to the ranch or wherever they saw her, in any place she wandered, when she picked wildflowers or at the village cemetery to take them to the grave of the old woman who cared for her since birth.

The beautiful young girl soon realized that nobody could stand her, which is why she rarely came to the ranch. The people of the ranch didn't care about the young girl anymore. Almost all were afraid of her, as even just looking at her, they believed something bad might happen to them. That's why nobody bothered her anymore. They didn't know what she ate or how she lived, whether she got sick, because she seemed healthy. Occasionally, she went to the dumps to find food scraps that others threw away. That's what she sometimes ate.

The sadness of abandonment, the misfortune of being an orphan and living alone, was very cruel and tormenting for her. It was difficult to live as she desired, but with effort and willpower, one could say that what she had, what she ate, and the little she lived on was not her desired life. It was barely enough to survive the cruel contempt and humiliation from everyone who knew her. Because sometimes, to eat, when she didn't come down to the community, to find something to eat, she had to learn to hunt to catch lizards, fish, and squirrels, which were all she ate out of the daily hunger she carried.

Like prey or a stray animal, she was abandoned again. She spent much of her sad life in depression and terrible loneliness, disappointed because she was envied and criticized for her beauty.

Prejudice condemned her to a miserable life, for she communicated with no one when she seldom went to the ranch or saw anyone. Only the ranch's crazy woman was her sole company, the only one who helped that poor girl with great kindness in every way possible. That crazy woman, who was also humiliated and mistreated, was the only one who visited her, gave her something to eat. Some people who feared her just watched her when she went out to visit the abandoned grave of the woman who once protected her, proudly jumping, insinuating she was singing. She was seen smiling, carrying field flowers in her apron, which she picked. Even though she bounced like a playful goat and shook all over, the flowers did not fall from her apron.

Possibly, her life, little or almost nothing, no longer mattered to her, because she spent almost all day embraced on the tomb of that old woman who cared for her. She was seldom seen in some parts she visited, seen fewer times. Only rarely did she go to the river to bathe or catch some fish, which was what little she ate to survive her hunger. With her soft hands, she caressed her perfect body with divine sensuality when bathing with wild gourds. When she left, some who saw her almost naked never forgot the scent she left and the memory of her body's beauty in their minds, seeing her bathe. The image stayed with them like an echo, but as they feared her, no man dared approach her or talk to her. Perhaps it was fear or maybe they were simply cowards who remained with their false prejudice, vanity, and foolish beliefs.

Perhaps she was too beautiful for them, and since she did not speak, they found it difficult to understand her because she never learned to speak or went to school. Even the teachers in those towns believed the gossip, and they too were complicit in criticizing and offending her. Like deranged cowards, they also mocked her. That was another reason why she never learned to read or write, so she couldn't communicate with them using letters.

She was always treated like a criminal or a mangy flea-ridden person by the people of that ranch. Perhaps because of a divine source, whenever she was in danger, something strange and powerful defended her from the coward's malice. They criticized her for it and even accused her of being a witch, condemning her to an even worse life. No one could or wanted to understand that she did not ask to have that power. She never realized that something mysterious saved her from cruelty, or even less, that she asked to be a pretty little girl, who, over time and years, became a beautiful young woman and later turned into a lovely, beautiful woman, one of her worst curses, condemned for the beauty of her body. Though men desired her, because of their foolish beliefs, they instead claimed to hate her. She had no one in her life to protect her, only that blessing from heaven that seemed to come to save her from danger when some deranged people wanted to take advantage of her.

Being so beautiful did not serve that young woman, as she barely interacted with anyone. She only associated with the crazy woman and a boy from that ranch, who, despite his parents forbidding him, went to the young woman's house and communicated with her through signs. Maybe that is why he accompanied her in moments of sadness because he felt happy with her or found being with her pleasant and fun. He didn't care if his parents were upset with him or punished him or forbade him. Thus, for a long time, they were the ones who kept company with the beautiful young woman, as the other villagers, with the fear they had of her and their prejudice, cowardly continued to condemn her. Perhaps the other people did not care about the beautiful abandoned young woman, and so she did not seek them out either. Possibly she also hated them with the same intensity in her heart, but with the boy's and the crazy woman's company, the three of them were happy, forgetting everything when they stayed together watching her pick wildflowers.

She was not the witch some people called her, nor was she the demon or as evil as they believed. She was rather a kind and charismatic young woman, a good person, but the foolishness of people, the superstition of ignorant people, who even today still believe in satanic witchcraft, spells, and whatever nonsense someone can think of and spread to other unbelievers, who are easily deceived. That is why they never wanted to understand that the young woman was kind and good. The boy and the crazy woman, who were very sure of this about the beautiful young woman, said it because she was very pleasant with them, never got angry with them, and always made an effort to be understood. Even the boy and the crazy woman seemed experts in that type of communication with signs and gestures, which was the way the beautiful young woman communicated with them. Additionally, as the boy and the crazy woman claimed, she was generous. She collected fruit and seeds from the fields and left them on the paths for someone to take. Many believed she forgot them there, threw them to the ground, and stepped on them so they would be useless, thinking they were doing her some harm, or they took them, thinking they were stealing them and that doing so would harm her.

People hardly wanted to talk about her, and the little they commented on was only to fill themselves with pride, speaking whatever nonsense came from their mouths. If someone mentioned her, it was only to insult her, which others followed like a litany, as if praying the rosary. For all who remembered her, it was more pleasant to insult her than to enjoy a good coffee or a cup of hot chocolate on a cold morning. The jealousy towards the beautiful young woman consumed the souls of dozens of women and young girls. That is why nobody cared about her, much less wanted her or accepted her into their lives, nor wanted to share anything with her or have her in their homes. When some people gave her something, like all cowards, they would throw it at her face or dress to mock her, without the slightest pity, because they all hated her and had no respect or compassion for her.

The contempt, mockery, curses, mistreatment, gossip, and whatever evil occurred to them never seemed to end, despite the fear they had of her. Nothing seemed to change, as the perversity in all who knew her ran through their veins like blood or a tattoo on their skin. They spoke of her with great resentment. But an unforgettable day, especially for a mother, had it not been for the young woman, who risked her life for a little child that, due to the mother's carelessness, almost drowned in the furious currents of the river. The mother was not watching when the currents carried her away, but the young woman, whom everyone humiliated, happened to be passing by, as she customarily did, and that was why she was there at the time. The mother was even more surprised because the young girl did not speak but shouted at the mother. When the mother tried to grab the little girl in the water, she slipped on a stone, and the current carried the baby further away. The mother went to rescue her little girl, but the strong currents dragged her too, and she could no longer see her daughter in the furious currents.

The woman who experienced the terrifying neglect and others who also saw it did not understand how the young woman they all cursed ran without thinking and threw herself into the strong water currents. She swam over them like a fish, grabbing and rescuing the girl several meters downstream. The mother was trapped between some rocks, holding onto branches, screaming for help because her life was in danger. Luckily for the mother, or maybe this was a lesson fate gave her, a great test, so she could reconsider her malice against the young woman who risked her life for her and her daughter, and they would no longer insult, mistreat, or curse her. At that moment, the crazy woman from the ranch passed by, looking for the beautiful young woman, and the young woman handed the girl to her while saving the mother and the girl from a cruel and merciless death.

Without caring for her life, she again threw herself into the wild currents of that raging river without caring that her life was in danger. Perhaps she thought her life was worthless for the furious river to take it. Without fear of death, she rescued the mother safely.

Love and affection, like all material things, sometimes also have a price. For this despised woman, she set a price on her life, a dangerous price she never imagined, which could have cost her her life if the wild currents of the furious river had dragged her and ended her life with its strong waters. She threw herself into the furious currents for something to happen in her life, for someone to at least thank her, and with some trust, little by little, she began to win over the lady she rescued from the furious currents and her family. This served her very little because, at the very least, this family stopped insulting or mistreating her, as they were the ones who humiliated her the most and mocked her when she approached their house or saw her pass by. But the love and the little trust they had placed in her lasted very little, as everyone hated the young woman so much that it didn't take long to convince them to despise her again and join in continuing to humiliate her and condemn her to the miserable life they all gave her.

The beliefs in those foolish, miserable villagers of that community and nearby ones were wicked and humiliating. They united to invent whatever prejudice or evil they could inflict on the humble young woman. Once again, they adorned her with a new slander, which greatly impacted the person who commented on it, passing it on to their other fools, who easily accepted it in their macabre brains and said it was true. They accused the poor young woman of the misfortune, having the ingenuity to say she was to blame for the child and the woman almost drowning. They said she did it to make them trust and forgive her, giving her time to plan more misfortunes against those who didn't believe it was a coincidence she was there, that she easily rescued the girl and the woman, and nothing happened to her, claiming it was the demon who helped her rescue them. Everything they invented was told to the family that almost drowned. They implored them to believe them, saying they only wanted to help her so that, cowardly, when they trusted her, she would take their lives. Their resentment towards the pretty young woman was so great that, after much insisting, they managed to convince them, and with that foolish belief, they remained.

It must be torturous and cruel for the people of those communities to carry so much hatred and contempt for the beautiful young woman in their souls, harboring all that perversity like poison in their veins and bodies, capable of such wicked infamies and slanders against the poor young woman. One day, due to another curse that befell that community, they accused the pretty young woman of being responsible for a disfigured creature being born and dying a few minutes after coming into the world. According to the villagers, she looked at the woman before the creature was born, and her presence beside her disfigured the fetus into a monster inside her womb, mocking the mother's pain when it was born.

To all the people of those ranches, the hatred and resentment they held for the beautiful young woman were like an epidemic, fed by the unjust slanders they invented. The contempt they had for her was more than the blood coursing through their veins. Some women decided to end her life, considering the birth of the disfigured child and its death sufficient reason to kill her. It was not only their excuse to take the young woman's life; some of them invented that the pretty young woman had been involved with their husbands, which is why they decided to confront her. But on the way, once again, the spirit of that old woman saved her, as that mysterious furious animal, transformed into an enraged coyote, blocked their path and did not let them pass. Frightened as snakes, they better retreated, like all cowards, reaching their homes and closing the doors with their offspring inside, fearing that the mysterious furious animal might swallow them if it was following them.

For this beautiful young woman, time and the malice against her never stopped. Due to the prejudices of foolish people, she even ended up in jail because some wicked people accused her of poisoning their animals. The cowards accused the defenseless, beautiful young woman of this evil act. The officers who arrested her, on orders from her accusers or perhaps out of cruelty or arrogance, tied her hands and feet, beat her with their weapons and kicks, and threw her into a truck like a true criminal, worse than a bag of trash. Like cowards, they drove away with her. The accusers celebrated as if it were a birthday or a trophy they had won, bringing beer cartons and celebrating for hours until they ran out of beer.

On the way, the fate of the defenseless poor young woman was not pleasant. Her destiny once again turned against her, and she was savagely humiliated. Her new misfortune was cruel and perverse, as the cowardly police officers continued to laugh and mock her, hypocritically celebrating and grabbing her intimate parts with malice. The wicked cowards laughed devilishly at how she was dressed, how she looked, and mocked her by hitting or spitting on her face.

The beautiful young woman was in jail for almost two weeks. Her life was miserable, and they humiliated her at will. They gave her little food or water, and the little she could drink, they threw in her face. They barely took care of her. Only one of the commanders entered her cell and maliciously stripped her clothes, slapping her face and body, demanding she tell the truth about the animals' poisoning. But like all cowards, he only mocked her, and when he left the cell, he threw her clothes at her face with hatred, satisfied with his savagery, leaving the cell while laughing. He often spat at her and told his colleagues not to feed her or give her anything to drink, to bathe her with dirty water so she would learn that no one mocked him.

The tortures inflicted on that young woman were immense. Her executioners, the commander, and two police officers spat on her face and body, beating her with their weapons against the wall every time they visited her cell, leaving her almost dead on the floor. None of the other police officers or staff who worked there, people who watched her being abused, had any compassion for her, even though they saw her being tortured. They all watched, but nobody cared, except for an old woman who cleaned the floors, who occasionally talked to her. But since the beautiful prisoner could not speak, she could not say anything, but the kind old woman would leave her a banana, fruit, or something to eat when the officers were not looking or were absent because they had threatened her with death if she gave her anything. It was the only food she ate, what the kind old woman could give her.

In grave condition from hunger and the ruthless tortures the beautiful woman suffered, she had to be taken to the emergency hospital on a doctor's orders. The old woman who cleaned the floors went to report her condition to the doctor, and without hesitation, the kind doctor went to the jail to rescue her. Without asking for permission, the doctor and the old woman went to see the fainted young woman in her cell. At that moment, the commander came out and angrily shouted at them not to approach her, but the doctor confronted him and said he had to go in and see her. He politely asked him to open the gate, but the commander became furious, trying to scare him away, but the doctor was not intimidated and insisted that if he didn't open the gate, he would report him to other authorities or human rights. The argument was heated. The commander told him to leave her there, to let her die like a cockroach or a rat because, to him, that's what the fainted young woman deserved. The commander, with rage or hatred, yelled at the doctor to get out, saying he had nothing to do with her to defend her, telling him to leave to ask the ranch people why nobody liked her or why they hated her.

The doctor was not a coward that the wicked commander could scare. He insisted that she be handed over because it was his duty to help her and cure her. The cowardly commander refused his request. The doctor, also very angry, asked him to release her voluntarily, either the easy way or the hard way. The commander became even more furious, pushing him, and with his police officers, they tried to remove him, but the doctor confronted them. Already upset and very annoyed, he repeated that they should open the gates or if anything worse happened to the fainted young woman, he would accuse them in federal court for injuries, physical harm, cruelty, and abuse against him and the young woman, in federal court and human rights. The commander, hypocritically, changed his voice, pretending not to be angry. He grabbed the doctor by the shoulder and walked him a few steps while saying in a supposedly friendly voice: "Doctor, this is not your problem, don't get involved, it's better for you to leave!" The doctor did not back down, removed his hand from his shoulder, and then, without fear, placed his hand on the commander's back and with the same fake voice and hypocrisy, pushed him towards the gate, saying in a low voice, almost in his ear, "Commander, open that gate! It's in your best interest, unless you want to end up locked up there or in another federal state jail." The commander returned to his original voice, with contempt, hatred, and anger, cursing the young woman and mistreating the doctor, raging like fighting rats, and opened the jail gate.

The doctor, seeing the beautiful prisoner lying on the dirty floor, ran without hesitation to the fainted young woman, lifted her slightly with his hands, placing her between his arms and legs, observing her a little, seeing her very faint. Without hesitation, and despite the commander and his police officers trying to stop him, without listening to them, he took her in his arms and carried her out of the dirty and cold cell, without a doubt, taking her to his car. The commander and his police officers, dying of rage, stayed in the jail, while the doctor drove at high speed without stopping until he reached his hospital, where other doctors were waiting for him. The doctor, risking his life and running over others, had called them on his cell phone, telling them he was heading to the hospital so they could be prepared. Several doctors and nurses awaited the fainted young woman, who was immediately admitted to an emergency room.

For a few days, the young woman was hospitalized in intensive care, gradually recovering from the cruel, ruthless martyrdom and torture she had endured. Meanwhile, the commander, along with his police officers, went after the poor old woman to take revenge. They went to find her where they knew how to locate her because they had fired her from her job as a sweeper in the jail. When they found her, they beat her for a few minutes until they murdered her, then threw her into a city sewer like a lagoon next to them, sure that no one saw them. That's what they thought, but they didn't realize that while their eyes didn't see, other eyes were watching them. Someone was there, watching when they came to dispose of the woman, but this person was hidden in a place the cowards didn't see and observed everything. But since they saw they were police officers, they were afraid and told no one.

In the hospital, the young woman was well cared for, as the doctors, nurses, and staff treated her with great love, patience, and respect. It was not difficult for them to communicate with her, as they used sign language, which the doctors and nurses knew and practiced.

One day, the cowardly commander, along with his police officers, came to the hospital, insisting on taking the abandoned young woman back to jail. The doctors and medical staff did not allow them to approach her, much less arrest her, leading to several confrontations with heated discussions between the commander, his police officers, and the medical staff within the hospital. They were determined to use force and exert their will. That's why one day, they tried to forcibly take the defenseless young woman under arrest. They entered her room and cowardly tried to handcuff her, but doctors, nurses, and other staff pushed and fought them off, forcing the commander and his officers out like mangy rats. However, the commander and his team, with offensive words, threatened all the medical staff, but they did not back down and, being cowards, threw them out into the street.

The conflicts between the medical staff and the commander and his aides did not end there. On another occasion, they again engaged in heated discussions, as they wanted to forcefully take the arrested young woman back to jail to pay for what she owed for what she had done. Some doctors asked how much she owed, saying they would pay it. The commander replied that it wasn't their problem, that none of them could help her, and that she had to pay her debt with jail time. With or without their permission, they intended to arrest her and take her to jail, where she should be locked up.

With great hatred in his soul, the commander sarcastically shouted for her to die there and then be thrown into a garbage dump or ravine. This angered the medical staff and security, who forced them out of the hospital. Another fight was unnecessary, and due to so much confrontation, the doctors decided, along with their lawyers, to sue the commander and his aides in federal court.

When the court day arrived, the commander and his team defended themselves, but the injuries, physical and mental harm inflicted on the young woman were recorded in medical records and photographs. With all this evidence, they accused the commander and his assistants of assault against medical staff, invasion and destruction with damage to property, and police abuse against citizens. The court also had relatives of the old woman who cleaned the floors, accusing them of her murder, as they already knew they had killed her.

The person who saw the commander and his police officers when they killed the old woman who cleaned the floors also came to court. They testified and accused them as well. Seeing they were cornered, one of the police officers whom the commander mistreated revealed the truth about the old woman's death. He told the court that he, along with his commander, intercepted her on a street. They struck her on the head, preventing her from defending herself, forcibly put her into their truck, took her to a nearby area, and beat her to death. The officer testified in court that he and his companion held her by her hands and feet, but it was the commander who beat her to death. As a result, the medical staff won the court case, and the young woman was released. The judge imposed a fine of nearly one hundred fifty thousand pesos, which the court would return when the case of the animal poisoning was investigated and clarified.

Those were blessed days for the unfortunate young woman, who, just weeks earlier, had everything against her, and it seemed like the end of her life due to the cruelties her body and soul had endured. That day and a few days before were beacons of light in her path. Finally, someone was able to help and understand her without humiliating or despising her. Those days were unforgettable for everyone, especially for the precious young woman, who was rescued from a cruel, cursed massacre when her life seemed to be ending.

Perhaps it was not her destiny to die at that moment. Her story was not over. Her suffering, martyrdom, curse, and calvary were far from ending, but at that moment, everything was a blessing, a respite for the deeply humiliated young woman. There were many people who cared for her during that time. Doctors, nurses, and other medical staff who attended the court quickly organized with the lawyers, raised money, and paid the fine. This is why they could take the beautiful young woman from there without detaining her. She now had a blessing in her life, as there were no more executioners to condemn her to a cruel and ruthless life. Her torturers were locked up in a cell at the court.

The accusers were accused; those who judged and condemned were judged and condemned. There in that court, the commander and his aides were arrested and taken to a cell within the court, where they were locked up as the cowards they were.

Once everything had ended, the doctors returned the young woman to the hospital to continue her recovery, as some of her wounds had not fully healed. Her weakness made her vulnerable to infections, which the doctors fought fiercely to save her from. They believed that if they hadn't treated her immediately, a day later could have been fatal for the young woman, possibly resulting in the amputation of her body parts or her death, as the miserable police officers would never have taken her to a hospital. Behind bars, where they had her locked up, her young life would have ended.

A few days later, the beautiful young woman had recovered, not completely, but at least her health was no longer in danger. Her physical problems had not fully healed, but the doctors assured her it was no longer necessary to stay there longer. Regarding the psychological issues caused by the terrible tortures she suffered, the doctors, specialists in that area, assured her it would be very difficult to erase them from her memories. Still, some swore to help her at least have someone to talk to, and if they could help her fully recover, it would be a significant achievement for them. They jokingly or motivationally said it would be a trophy they would win. Seeing the young woman's problems, they had no doubt it would be difficult to achieve her complete recovery. It would be incredible and a great pride for them and the beautiful young woman, who would no longer suffer that condemnation in her soul. At the same time, they were aware of the harassment problems from her community and nearby ranches, fully aware of the evil she suffered from them. Out of affection and compassion, they were all willing to help her without expecting anything in return, without her asking, begging, or imploring them. Their services were offered out of a willingness to serve those in need, and there was no doubt she needed them, which is why they decided to help her without setting any conditions.

Not only were the psychologists willing to help the beautiful young woman, but everyone who assisted her recovery in the hospital also committed to continuing to help her whenever needed. The nurses were willing to continue visiting her to assist with any health issues. The lawyers who defended her also promised to conduct a thorough investigation into the animal poisoning case that led to her imprisonment and torture in the cell where the psychopaths guarding her were the executioners who subjected her to severe punishments. The lawyers promised to find the true cause of the alleged animal poisoning, stating that if it were false, those who accused her would have to pay for the evil they did. They assured her that they would make them regret the evil done to the young woman. If they falsely accused her to have her imprisoned, those who offended her would end up locked up, as clarified to the police, who proudly said: just like the police who arrested her and took her away.

Now, the beautiful young woman didn't have just one person to help her. Everyone who got to know her in a short time, including doctors, nurses, lawyers, and more medical staff, was willing to help, defend, and care for her. She was no longer alone, having the affection of many who knew her and sympathized with her kindness and pain. Out of their desire to help and as part of their profession, for which they had specialized, they all united without setting any obstacles or conditions.

Since everyone who met her knew she wouldn't return to jail, there were now people who cared about her. All the doctors, nurses, and lawyers offered her a home before telling her she no longer needed treatment there. They expressed their desire in sign language, as almost everyone understood that form of communication for people with speech impairments. They told her to stay with them, and she explained, as best she could, that she couldn't stay because she had to take care of the grave of the woman who cared for her when she was a baby. They told her it wasn't a problem and that someone from among them would take her whenever she wanted, but she didn't accept their invitations. They understood her and were concerned about her because of it.

Even though everyone offered her a home, she did not accept it. No matter how much they insisted, she accepted nothing from anyone. Others offered her a job so she could work, have her own money, buy clothes, new shoes, and everything she could purchase. They would provide her with food in their homes, but it was crucial for them that she decided to stay due to the danger she would face in that community. She replied that she was already used to being mocked and humiliated, but the immense love she had for the woman who cared for her as a child was more important than anything they did to her, even if they killed her.

Drenched in her salty tears, the beautiful, abandoned young woman couldn't stop crying. Everyone was surprised, almost in shock, like robots, with the explanations she gave them. To everyone, it seemed that all those words she explained were very emotional to believe that such expressions came from that young woman. Some thought she had learned them but wondered how she had learned them when she was left alone as a baby because no one could have taught her to express herself that way or remember them. It was impossible for them to believe it, seeming as if they were written in a Bible she was merely reading to make them understand.

The people accompanying her in her room told her they were willing to help her return with them. They said everyone would help, and to prevent boredom from staying in one place, she could spend time with one person and then with another. They did not want her to return to danger where harm could befall her. She replied that she didn't care if she were killed; she would stop suffering, and her soul would reunite with the old woman, believing that the old woman still remembered and would want and help her again.

In her heart, soul, and spirit, the young woman desired to be free as the wind, like squirrels or any other wild animal, only wishing to run around. Maybe that's why she decided not to have anyone care for her since she was a baby. Her happiness was feeling like flying like birds, imagining raising her wings and setting out on a journey across all horizons, crossing valleys and mountains, rivers, and lakes without getting wet. She grew up free, which was why she couldn't be in a cage, even if it were made of gold or beautiful crystals with fine diamonds. She didn't want to be inside it, as confinement could be a fearful fate that might end her beautiful wild life. Despite all the martyrdom and severe and cruel torture she endured, her soul was happy.

The beautiful, abandoned young woman was already desperate, which is why she wanted to leave. While still sitting on her bed, everyone talked to her, or rather cried, as tears rolled down from their eyes. They communicated with her through sign language, as almost everyone understood that form of communication. This made it easy for her to understand them, despite her attempts to stand up or walk away from where she was seated. They didn't let her leave the hospital.

The beautiful young woman let out the cry from within her wounded soul. Everyone communicated with her; some tried to hold back their sobs but couldn't resist. They admired the young woman's bravery and the love she held for the old woman who cared for her as a baby. Some embraced her, and the lovely young woman tried to break free, but they didn't let go because of their immense affection for her. Perhaps no one was willing to let her go, which is why they pleaded with her to stay. They all felt that the young woman they were helping deserved a beautiful life, which is why they offered it to her. Their kindness towards the young woman was incredible; they admired each other, as their souls and profession placed them in this destiny to help those in need, and the beautiful young woman had already stolen their noble hearts. To them, the needs of that lovely young woman were not an exception, so they decided to help her in any way possible. But when they gave up, realizing they couldn't keep her, they saw that she was about to leave. They noticed that no one convinced her to stay with them, so they asked her to wait and that some of them wanted to accompany her to her ranch.

After almost three hours of trying in vain to stop her and convince her to stay with them, they realized they would not succeed despite their pleas and supplications. Some of them left the hospital without even going home, those who said they had no one waiting for them. Some joked that not even lice or cockroaches awaited them because they didn't even have those. Others, slightly comforted, still had tears on their cheeks from the sobs that had escaped and continued to escape, saying amidst their sobs that they didn't have even a dog or a cat to howl or bark at them as they accompanied her.

Shortly after some extra sighs and sobs that wouldn't stop coming from their souls, a few minutes later, once they decided who would go with her, they began to leave the hospital halls to start their departure to that ranch where they would leave the young woman, the beautiful young woman who had stolen their hearts and left many sighs and memories with everyone who knew her.

It seemed nobody wanted to start the departure; they hesitated not because they didn't want to help the young woman but because they feared what might happen to her. They were sure that sooner or later, due to their work and needs, they would have to leave her. That's why perhaps nobody dared to begin the journey, as, in reality, nobody wanted to in their souls. Everyone wished that young woman would stay with them to be safe from those depraved diabolical monsters, without worrying about being harmed.

Already in the parking lot, believing and hoping she would stay, they continued talking, but the lovely young woman was desperate. Knowing how to communicate in sign language, she insisted they leave and start the journey. Feeling pressured by the young woman's demands, they began to get into their cars and set off in a convoy, with some of the people accompanying her in their vehicles.

Once on the road, after departing, the pleas and requests of those kind, charismatic people who drove her did not cease. From the bottom of their hearts, they wished she would stay with one of them. On the way, they insisted, asking if she would return with them, but she said no because she had to take flowers to the grave of the old woman who cared for her when she was a child. She was sure that the grave needed wildflowers, and she wished to bring them.

On dusty and ugly roads, after almost an hour of travel, they felt a bit relieved to have reached their destination, feeling they had fulfilled part of their promise. However, the surprise they encountered was unpleasant and cruel, as the house where the helpless beautiful young woman lived was destroyed and burned. The wicked, cowardly people had burned it with wood from the field, demolishing its remaining old walls. Seeing what had happened, everyone, including the lovely young woman and the visitors, was shocked. The precious young woman burst into tears at the overwhelming, miserable pain she felt upon seeing the old house destroyed.

The visitors felt cruel pain witnessing the destruction of the abandoned young woman's refuge. They remained stunned, filled with anger and courage, commenting on what had happened, what they saw with their own eyes, confirming that those wicked people, with a great force of cowardly instincts, seemed to want to destroy her. They imagined they wanted to kill her, as that was what the wicked desired in their dens, with a thirst for the tremendous hatred they felt towards her, waiting for her arrival.

The beautiful young woman, seeing her house reduced to ashes, burst into tears, using her little hands and tear-filled eyes, murmuring as tears fell on her pretty mouth. It seemed like she was speaking, seeing the cruelty inflicted upon her. The lovely young woman couldn't contain herself, as the immense pain in her deeply wounded soul received yet another profound wound, further destroying her. Unable to stop crying from the terrible pain caused, she nearly fainted. While some looked around, they couldn't understand the malice and hatred directed towards the young woman. The little they saw confirmed that those visitors had no doubt that those people were not human. They thought that, like a pack of hungry wolves, they attacked her. Hungry wolves were an understatement of what they truly were, for they were human carrion, monsters made of evil.

The truth was that those visitors were not wrong. The ranch cowards said the young woman was a cursed witch, protected by the devil, and should be sacrificed and killed in the most cowardly way their deranged minds could conceive. However, they were the true demons, serpents stalking their prey, ready to swallow her at the slightest slip. The beautiful young woman and her companions, who were with her at the time, never imagined that something diabolical in that ranch filled with cowardly murderers and cruel wickedness was being planned against the helpless young woman.

The human wolves had already seen her arrive, so they began preparing, spreading rumors among themselves that they would torture her, make her cry for forgiveness and mercy for what she did, lynch her, then burn her so the devil could see how one of his emissaries, one of his souls on this earth, died. They accused her again, despite her absence, blaming her for something unrelated to the lovely young woman, claiming she was responsible for a child's foot rotting from gangrene and dying hours after birth. Similarly, they said some piglets were born with the same deformity. They declared that what happened there was the work of the devil, and for them, the only devil among them was the lovely young woman they hated with great fervor. That day, when the beautiful young woman returned to the ranch, everyone, without exception, was prepared and anxious to make her pay for her supposed deserved punishment, waiting for her as they proudly blamed her for the curse, which the poor young woman had nothing to do with.

The monsters had their plan ready, eager to execute it and quench their diabolical thirst, but they couldn't carry it out that day. In rage, they walked in packs, cursing and swearing at the visitors with the beautiful young woman. For those wicked perverts, failing to execute their evil plan was another sign that the devil was with her, or she was the devil, so the visitors didn't leave her alone. To the misfortune of those diabolical ranchers, the young woman's visitors had no plans to leave her alone, something they didn't know. Therefore, that day, the young woman's visitors were there, but the agreement among those savage perverts was to act when the visitors left. They rubbed their hands and tongues in desperation, unable to carry out their wicked execution.

Among all the visitors, they comforted the previously abandoned young woman, trying to calm her down, but her pain was immense, a tremendous punishment in her noble soul that was difficult to control, cruel and perverse suffering that was hard to bear. Her visitors couldn't help her with this martyrdom, but seeing her pain, misery, tears, and immense desperation, they promised to build her a new house. They were all trying to help her.

Some of them went to the ranch to ask for help, but they received an unpleasant surprise. Everyone they asked for help angrily told them that no one would help, some with extreme malice, even cursing her, saying it was the least that demon deserved, that nobody wanted to see her, and everyone hated her, so nobody would help her.

Those visitors who went to ask for help returned with resentment, anguish, and anger at not being able to get anything. Everyone was upset because they couldn't believe the hatred directed towards the poor beautiful young woman. So they had to return to where the young woman and the others were waiting. When the others saw them arrive empty-handed, they became very sad. After hearing everything they said, they were even more surprised than before, contemplating what to do and commenting on their suspicions that people hated the helpless young woman. They thought that something terrible could happen to her, something serious would occur if they left her alone.

The danger the beautiful young woman faced by being left alone seemed to dawn on the visitors. They realized that those people were not human as they saw, heard, and expressed themselves. They judged her, murmured about her, and condemned her. The demons, the monstrous devils, were those people from the community and other nearby ranches who knew the humble young girl.

It was terrifying for all the young woman's visitors; they believed it was too dangerous to leave her alone, something they might regret for their lives and lament for having abandoned her. Seeing they couldn't help her, everyone insisted she return with them, stay with whoever she wanted, in any house she wanted. She told them no, she would stay because she had to bring flowers to the grave of the old lady who had taken care of her when she was little. Even so, they insisted, telling her to leave with them, that she didn't have a house to sleep in there, that nobody wanted her, that everyone despised her, and that they were sure something unfortunate would happen to her if they left her alone. She told them she wasn't leaving, and if she didn't have a house, she would sleep on the ground. If not, she would go to the grave of the old woman who took care of her and stay on top of it. The visitors told her she had no blanket, no clothes, nor anything to cook with. They insisted that the inhabitants of the ranch hated her, that they didn't want her. She told them she didn't care, she already knew, and that nobody wanted her, but it was important for her to visit and bring flowers from the field to the grave of the old lady she adored so much.

The beautiful young woman, even in her cruel pain, could not stop crying, with her salty tears falling into her mouth. She expressed in sobs that even though she was no longer with her, she would never forget her, and it felt as if she were inside her soul. The visitors, moved by her even more, admired the kindness of this beautiful young girl whom everyone criticized, judged, and maliciously condemned. No one could resist crying and sobbing again; some joined her in crying with despair and anguish. Others, a little closer, could not resist the suffering and pain they felt in their souls for that young woman. It was hard for them to believe the reasons for which those wicked people accused her.

For a long while, everyone said they understood her immense affection for the old lady, whom she said had taken care of her when she was a child. Although they all pleaded with her to take her away, she wouldn't decide. They promised to take her and bring her back to see the old lady's grave whenever she wanted, yet they couldn't convince her to leave with them because nobody wanted to leave her alone. They felt sure that something serious would happen to her.

The young woman's visitors felt pity, sadness, anguish, and desperation. They were terrified of leaving her alone, sensing that something would happen to her from the wicked people in the town. They all thought that if something happened because they left her alone, they would feel guilty. That's why they hinted at it and insisted she go with them because they might kill her. She continued to refuse, saying no, she wouldn't go. Nearly fainting from crying and sadness, she told them through gestures and murmurs that if they killed her, perhaps that would be better because she would stop suffering and being hated so much for reasons she didn't know. She said she had done nothing to make anyone hate her or despise her with anger and hatred. The visitors' eyes filled with salty tears, which ran down to their chests, from the sadness they felt for the defenseless young woman. This was yet another sign that the visitors could see that the beautiful young woman was noble, kind, and had love to give. They thought the affection she had for the old lady, after so many years, was admirable. Some commented that very few children had such great affection for their mothers. Together with her, they hugged each other, unable to do anything if the young woman wouldn't go with them, fearing a tragedy when they returned to their work.

For a long time, they pondered what to do. Nobody wanted to leave, and no one wanted to leave her alone. So when night fell, they all lay down, surrounded by a fire, and when morning came, she left the field without them. Some who saw her leaving followed her to see where she was going, to ensure no one approached her with ill intent. They were relieved when they saw her happy, picking wildflowers with her delicate hands in her dress. They watched her simulate singing joyfully. With flowers in her dress, they saw her take a path to a road. They joined her, and those who stayed informed the others they were going to the cemetery to bring flowers to the old lady's grave she visited.

A few hours later, those who had gone to the cemetery with the precious young woman returned. They all seemed happy with the young woman, even forgetting their work. Together with her, they went to pick more wildflowers, to visit the old lady's grave and leave the flowers they had gathered. The kind visitors, with immense affection, again accompanied her in their cars. For a long while, some walked around the cemetery, while others stayed close to the defenseless young woman. Since she arrived, she lay face down on the old lady's grave, crying as if telling her of her pain. Some companions stayed close without saying anything until after a long time when the young woman seemed to have fallen asleep. She woke up, and all the visitors were already together. They asked if she was ready to leave, and she said yes, again with them to where she returned to her house.

Afterward, they went to buy food at another ranch, thinking that if they went to the ranch where the beautiful young woman lived, they might not sell anything. So at the other ranch, they bought food, pots, blankets, and everything they could buy. When they returned to the ranch where the defenseless young woman lived, the visitors seemed not to remember anything, happily cooking together. After finishing, they ran through the fields, bathed in the river, searched for crabs under rocks, or looked for fish, enjoying themselves. Some passed the time, while others went to see her, walking through the fields with her. They admired her when they saw her happily murmuring as she sang, picking wildflowers.

They all feared something terrible would happen to the young woman and couldn't find a way to convince her since she didn't want to leave with them, nor did they want to leave her alone. While pondering what to do, they looked for distractions until they decided someone should stay with her. But the problem was who would stay with her. Some older nurses decided to stay with her for a few days since they had no family waiting for them or a little dog to bark at them. They thought nobody would miss them, but they would bring clothes, food, and everything needed to settle in and quickly gather enough money or material to build another house for the beautiful young woman who was once again defenseless.

So everyone left, leaving only the two women behind. But some people from the town watched from afar, seeing she wasn't alone, and once again, the wicked couldn't execute their plan. With the same anger they felt the day before when the visitors accompanied her, they stayed behind, seething like wounded wild wolves. Early the following day, they had visitors: the boy who used to accompany her and the crazy woman from the ranch. The two were very happy to see her, embracing like joyful children and shouting and jumping around until one of them slipped and all three fell to the ground. They stood up, dusted off their clothes, and the nurses who stayed with the young woman were surprised at how much they loved each other. They were surprised and happy, but at the same time, they wondered why the boy and the woman loved her so much when everyone else in the ranch treated her so cruelly and hated her. But they felt good seeing them leave, still shouting and jumping with joy for having reunited. They watched them, shoulders held together, and followed them closely, confirming how happy she was with the boy and the crazy woman from the ranch. They didn't interrupt them, just watched from a distance when she gathered wildflowers with them.

While the beautiful young woman picked wildflowers, the boy and the crazy woman looked for grasshoppers because they liked to play with them. They spent a long time that way until they saw a small rabbit they wanted to catch. When the crazy woman tried to catch it, the rabbit ran, and they had to follow it. The young woman left her flowers on the ground to help them, but even with the three of them, they couldn't catch it. Several times they fell while trying to catch it, and sometimes they scraped their feet and hands, but despite their efforts, they couldn't catch it. One of the nurses who had followed them told them to leave and told the boy to go home because his parents were likely looking for him. The boy was obedient and tried to leave.

It was true; the boy's parents were looking for him, arriving where they were. The parents started scolding him, but at the same time, they insulted the poor defenseless young woman with extremely offensive words. They said whatever came out of their mouths. Seeing the injustice and how they were mistreating the boy and the defenseless beautiful young woman with vile, offensive words, one of the nurses kindly asked them not to insult them. But the boy's parents rudely told the nurse to stay out of it, that it wasn't her problem, and to shut up. However, since she expressed herself well, she again asked them to calm down.

Those people, like rabid beasts, gradually complied, albeit unwillingly, and left, but not before insulting the nurse and the defenseless young woman again, who burst into tears and hugged the crazy woman from the ranch. The nurse also embraced them and asked them to calm down, jokingly saying that the demons had left.

She playfully made crosses with her fingers on the ground to encourage them to calm down. The two laughed while sobbing, playing and shouting with joy for a good while, playing and picking wildflowers in the fields.

The next day, a little late, the doctor arrived, the one who had rescued her from the abusive police officers who had her in jail. Three male nurses and two more female nurses came with him, bringing three men with a truck full of construction materials to build a house for the lovely defenseless young woman. A few minutes later, more nurses arrived, bringing the nurses' belongings. When the young woman saw them arriving, she ran to meet them, shouting and jumping like a little girl. When the doctor got out of his car, she ran to him, knocking him to the ground. There on the ground, like a playful child, she gave him several kisses on his cheeks and face before standing up and leaving the doctor on the ground until he could get up by himself.

The beautiful young woman stood up and did the same with all the nurses, but she didn't knock them to the ground. They were surprised to see her happiness at seeing them. They, in turn, made her feel happy and told her they were very proud of her, wishing her to feel better and telling her they would build her house as promised. Not without first inviting her again to go with them, she replied with gestures as always, saying no, she wouldn't go because she had to pick wildflowers to bring to the grave of the old lady who took care of her when she was a child.

With conversation, laughter, jokes, joy, playing, and shouting, the afternoon passed without notice. It was almost dark when they remembered they had to work to unload the material they had brought. Some didn't want to help; those with little will got up from where they were sitting or lying on the ground. But they decided to unload the material from the truck together quickly. However, as it was late, they didn't start building the house. They thought it was best to begin early the next day. Some nurses went to the river while the nurses prepared something for dinner. This time, they didn't cook with a wood fire; they cooked on a gas stove they brought.

As night fell, they all prepared to rest, sleeping on air mattresses and mats, while others slept on the ground. The next day, at sunrise, they woke up, and the men they had brought as builders, with the help of the doctor and nurses, began the project they had come for. Meanwhile, the nurses quickly prepared breakfast and lunch. After lunch, the nurses took the lovely young woman, telling her to come with them to buy clothes and other things for her to wear. They also took the woman, the beautiful young girl's friend. All day they entertained them at the stores, but before taking them and starting to build the house, they again asked her to please go with them, that they wanted her to go with them or someone among them. The answer was the same as always: no. Seeing her refusal, they took the beautiful defenseless young woman, and they began to build the house. Since it wasn't made of brick walls, they finished it that same day, making the walls and roof from steel sheeting, with wooden supports.

Before the new night fell, the house was finished, built for that beautiful young woman so hated by the townspeople. Upon finishing, they called her on the phone to bring her, but they called other companions to come. It didn't take long for them to arrive since the city where they went wasn't very far. When they arrived with the beautiful young woman, she stood, excited to see her new house, crying tears of joy and emotion. She hugged them again, giving each one dozens of kisses. No one escaped her kisses and hugs. Crying as she could, she thanked them repeatedly with gestures. The crazy woman from the ranch was there, for she had also been invited. She also cried with emotion when the lovely young woman asked if she wanted to live with her in her new house. The visitors also asked the crazy woman to stay with the beautiful defenseless young woman in the new house. The crazy woman, rubbing her eyes, grabbing her face, and pulling her hair, excitedly said yes, she would stay with her, crying with joy, saying that now she wouldn't have to sleep on the streets or in garbage dumps. Still emotional and sobbing, wiping the tears from her eyes with her hands, she pointed with one hand to the corner where she wanted to sleep. Everyone laughed and asked the lovely young woman if she would give her that corner. She replied yes, and they said that from that moment on, that corner was hers.

A few hundred meters away from there, the hours and days seemed to pass too slowly for those wicked people. They anxiously awaited the moment to carry out their macabre and diabolical plan. The residents of that village thought the visitors of the beautiful young woman had stayed too long. They wished they would leave so they could commit their dreadful crime. They were like wolves enraged in a cage, even worse than caged wolves that hadn't eaten for weeks, waiting for the moment to tear apart and finish off their prey, to satisfy their hunger with the victim. Desperate and angry, they were furious that the strangers hadn't left. The wolves were anxious and felt a thirst for revenge, a pointless vengeance of which the precious young woman was never aware. It never crossed her mind, the unpleasant curse that occurred there, of which she was innocent but was cowardly accused. Much less could she imagine what the wicked people of the village were planning against her. But like rabid wolves howling, they swallowed the same hatred they had for her again because the visitors hadn't left.

The fun among the young woman's visitors, with her, and the hours and days they spent together were sweet, like the honey from the flowers the beautiful young woman picked in the fields. They wandered through the fields and rivers, like children or flying birds. Their shouts and laughter could be heard from afar. They climbed trees, slid down hills, gathered fruits from the field, and collected colorful stones on the river beaches or in the fields. They did hundreds of things to pass the time having fun. Everything was a game, fun, and joy for them, so they spent the whole day happy. Some went out to the dusty streets of the village to buy a drink or to try to make friends with the people, but they were met with cowardly disappointment. Some people wouldn't answer them, while others got up from their chairs or benches, acting as if they saw lepers or filthy people, ignoring them completely. Even the shopkeeper would hide to avoid selling them anything.

It seemed that those visitors had also become targets of the hatred and contempt, the curses wished upon the lovely young woman, who was insulted whenever they saw her. This is why they were mistreated when they came to the village to buy something to eat or drink.

Discontented or disappointed, they returned to continue playing in the rivers or the fields and forgot the insults and contempt they had received. They even forgot they had to return to work in the city, as they were having such a good time. But when they returned to the reality of departure, they found reasons to stay. Some left, but others stayed, and this enraged the diabolical wolves because they couldn't carry out the hunt they desired. Their macabre, diabolical plan, the feast they were waiting for, couldn't be devoured or completed, and this made them even angrier. It was like a drug they were addicted to but couldn't use or afford to buy. For those diabolical people, the more time passed without the young woman's visitors leaving, the more cruel their macabre plan became.

The young woman's visitors stayed with her for almost three weeks. Some left, others came. Life in the fields or rivers was very pleasant for them. The echo of the hills and their animals bore witness to their joy. Some had never been in the fields, eaten wild fruits, or bathed in a river's current. Everything they saw was beautiful and fun. It was like new blood in their veins. They said it was a new life, freedom, fresh air to breathe and live, like living a fantasy from a movie, being asleep and having a dream they experienced. A dream they couldn't have while working and living in the city. They couldn't enjoy the happiness found in the fields or rivers. They shouted like lost madmen that the air they breathed there was health, life, happiness.

For all the young woman's visitors, it was a new world where they were enjoying themselves, but their joy was not shared by the diabolical wolves, who continued with the intention of carrying out their macabre plan. Some were too anxious, thirsty for blood, hungry to destroy the defenseless young woman, the prey they so desired to devour. She did nothing to them, but the diabolical wolves of that village, because of their foolish prejudices, made her guilty. That's why they wanted to repay the supposed debt with her life, cowardly lynching her. But it was a blessing for the precious young girl and a curse for the wolves, who besieged her with that hatred running through their veins. Like hungry wolves drooling, they remained with the desire once more.

As every date arrives or every saint has its day, the date for those malevolent, ruthless people of that village was approaching. The diabolical wolves who stalked the defenseless young woman, along with the other wicked ones from other communities who joined the hunt, commented in their meetings or conversations that they would have patience. The feast they desired would be more enjoyable, and they would have more eagerness to do their evil because the time was approaching. Little by little, the young woman's visitors were leaving her alone. The ruthless wolves already sensed the scent of their prey in the air, the taste of blood on their lips, in their mouths. They already sensed the feast they would enjoy, the banquet they would devour, the pleasure they would derive from watching her suffer. That was their macabre, diabolical plan. They didn't want to kill her with bullets or knives. Their pride was in capturing her alive because the pleasure they would derive was watching her plead for mercy, hearing her scream and cry in pain. In their diabolical brains, they had engraved the form of cruelty they would inflict, the ruthless way they would watch her agonize and die slowly.

It was a perverse agony they wanted to inflict on the beautiful young woman, which would be too cruel for her. Some wolves, thirsty for their vengeance, had the necessary tools to cause her pain. They imagined watching her die slowly in pain, imagining her lying as they wished, destroyed as they desired, bleeding like a freshly killed rabbit torn apart by coyotes or enraged dogs. Their resentment and hatred were so great that their imagination was insufficient. But united, they felt sure they would celebrate with a victorious feast.

The macabre, diabolical plan of those wicked people in the village arrived in the afternoon, a few hours before nightfall. Three of the young woman's last companions left, and she was left alone because two of them felt dehydrated. The temperatures were very high during those days, and they weren't accustomed to those conditions or had any medicines or remedies to control themselves. That's why the third had to take them, leaving the young woman alone. This was the opportunity the diabolical wolves seized. When they saw the young woman's visitors leave, they gathered in one of their houses to plan where to find her.

It seemed that the wicked monsters of that village felt incapable of capturing the humble, defenseless young girl because several other diabolical murderers from other villages also joined them. Men and women joined the hunt, planning where to search for her and how many groups to form to ensure she wouldn't escape. They had already reserved the place for her death. For them, the most challenging part was finding her because, as they said, she was protected by the demon who might help her escape, preventing their cruel instincts of vengeance from being realized. Some diabolical people thought the hunt would be simple because they knew where to find her and were familiar with the places the defenseless young woman visited. But others weren't so sure it would be easy to capture her, so they asked for help in other villages.

More than three hundred perverse diabolical monsters joined the hunt, along with trained tracking dogs. Others didn't go after her, but they were on standby to capture her. They stayed behind as relief for those who grew tired or were injured during the hunt or if something happened. When the sun began to set, dozens of groups of men, women, and some children went to different places to hunt her like real wolves thirsty for blood and evil, scouring all the fields, rivers, and mountains.

But they hadn't counted on the crazy woman from the village warning the beautiful defenseless young woman about the macabre plan the diabolical wolves had for her. That's why, when they went to hunt her, they searched along the path and the abandoned house where she lived, but they didn't see her. Like vultures, they went to the places the young woman visited, but unfortunately for them, they didn't find her. But for her, it was a blessing that she wasn't there. They communicated via cell phones that no one had found her, which made them feel even more furious and hateful. In each group, even with trained dogs, they searched desperately through the hills, mountains, rivers, pastures, and nearby towns, looking for her under rocks, in bushes, without rest. Although it was already night, many didn't care, their thirst for vengeance possessing them like demons. With flashlights and lanterns in the darkness, they searched everywhere for the defenseless young woman, but they couldn't find her. In anger, rage, and arrogance, they destroyed everything in their path.

The new house where the defenseless young woman lived was once again completely destroyed by those diabolical beasts, along with everything the young woman had, which her visitors had given her. They tore her clothes and burned them, as if with diabolical joy, celebrating a victory in a tournament, taking great pleasure in their destruction. They shouted angrily, destroying and burning everything the beautiful young woman had. In their shouts, one could hear the insults they hurled at her and the great pleasure they would take in finding her. Even the place where she picked flowers from the field was cowardly destroyed without mercy with machetes, sticks, and stomping.

The hours for those ruthless people, transformed into true wolves of the devil, thirsty for blood, were agonizing. It seemed like a mockery not to find her, which frustrated and infuriated them even more. Filled with hatred and desperation, they searched centimeter by centimeter through the fields and the river. When they couldn't find her in those places, they went to other villages, questioning every person they encountered. Fortunately for the young woman, no one told them they had seen her. Luckily for the beautiful, defenseless young woman, they didn't find her. They soon realized that maybe the beautiful young woman had sought refuge in a place unknown to them, a place only the crazy woman and the beautiful young woman knew. Indeed, it was a secret place to them. There, along with her, the young woman spent almost two nights and days, but at night, they would cautiously leave their hiding place to search for wild fruits and water to live or at least survive. They were aware of the danger they were in, terrified for their lives, and scared of being found.

The frustration for the people of the village, who like true hungry wolves didn't cease their hunt, was overwhelming. Day and night, they searched in dark and hidden places, lurking like cowards. They didn't want to lose the chance to catch her, feeling certain they would find her, even if they found her dead from thirst or hunger. They were confident that she would come out to search for water or food, and like a helpless rabbit, those ruthless vultures would hunt her. They mocked what awaited the poor young woman, saying among themselves that wherever she was hiding, she would eventually come out, perhaps dying of thirst or hunger, making her easier to catch.

They claimed she would come out even if she were in hell with the demon. Their desperation, anger, and frustration at not finding her led some to insinuate that she was Satan's lover, the demon's beloved, that the precious young woman prostituted herself even with the devil, and that's why he helped and hid her.

The people from the village continued their hunt, relentless and merciless, driven by an unfounded hatred that consumed them. Their plan was to catch her alive so they could torture her, savor her pain, and watch her suffer. It was a sadistic pleasure they longed for, an obsession that blinded them to reason or compassion. They saw the beautiful young woman not as an innocent girl but as a scapegoat for all their frustrations and anger, a victim to be sacrificed to quench their thirst for blood and revenge.

Days turned into nights and nights into days, yet their search was in vain. The beautiful young woman remained hidden, her whereabouts unknown to her pursuers. The crazy woman, her unlikely ally, stayed by her side, offering comfort and support. They lived in constant fear, knowing they were hunted, but they also knew they had to survive, if only to defy the wickedness that sought to destroy them.

The villagers, consumed by their hatred, grew more desperate with each passing day. They intensified their efforts, spreading their search farther and wider, determined to find their prey. But the beautiful young woman, with the help of the crazy woman, managed to stay one step ahead, eluding their grasp and evading capture.

The village was a place of fear and hatred, where innocence was punished and cruelty was celebrated. The beautiful young woman had done nothing to deserve the hatred directed at her, yet she was hunted as if she were the vilest of criminals. Her only crime was her beauty and innocence, qualities that should have been cherished but instead made her a target for the villagers' malice.

As the days dragged on, the young woman's strength began to wane. The constant fear and stress took their toll on her body and spirit. She longed for peace and safety, for a place where she could live without fear of being hunted. But she knew she had to keep going, to keep fighting, if not for herself, then for the memory of the old woman who had cared for her, for the love and kindness that still existed in the world.

The villagers, meanwhile, grew more frenzied in their pursuit, their hatred consuming them completely. They had become monsters, driven by an insatiable thirst for blood and revenge. They could not see the humanity in the beautiful young woman, blinded by their own evil intentions.

The beautiful young woman and the crazy woman continued to evade capture, moving stealthily from place to place, always on the run. They knew they could not hide forever, but they also knew they had to keep trying, to keep fighting against the darkness that sought to consume them.

The villagers, unable to find their prey, began to turn on each other, their hatred and anger eating away at their sanity. They blamed one another for their failure, their unity crumbling as their search proved fruitless. The beautiful young woman had become a symbol of their failure, a reminder of the darkness within themselves.

As the hunt dragged on, the beautiful young woman and the crazy woman found solace in each other's company, a bond forged in the crucible of fear and danger. They knew they had to rely on each other if they were to survive, if they were to overcome the evil that pursued them.

In the end, it was not the villagers who triumphed but the beautiful young woman and the crazy woman, their spirit and determination a testament to the strength of the human spirit. They had faced unimaginable horrors and had emerged victorious, their courage and resilience a beacon of hope in a world overshadowed by darkness.

The villagers, defeated and broken, were left to confront the darkness within themselves, their hatred and malice a reflection of the evil they had sought to inflict on the beautiful young woman. They had been consumed by their own wickedness, their humanity lost in the pursuit of revenge.

The beautiful young woman and the crazy woman, though scarred by their ordeal, found peace and safety in each other's company, their bond a testament to the power of love and friendship. They had survived the hunt, their strength and courage a shining example of the resilience of the human spirit.

Just as they had already thought, they seemed like bounty hunters who knew everything. They knew very well how to set the traps, the weapon that would serve them best, and they knew very well that the women were thirsty and hungry, something that neither people nor animals can endure for too long. It was this weapon that, unfortunately for her and the crazy woman from the ranch, led to their misfortune. That day arrived for her to pay the debt for which she was accused, just as the ruthless people of that village had planned. The beautiful, defenseless young woman, along with the crazy woman who accompanied her, came out from where they were hiding one not-so-dark night because the heat inside their hiding place was unbearable, and they were already dying of thirst. Nearby was a stream from which they drank water, but that day, to their misfortune, they were seen. When the cowards saw them coming, they emerged from their hiding spots. There were about eleven of the cowards who tried to catch them. They didn't want them dead; they wanted them alive because their plan was to lynch and torture the poor defenseless young woman. Killing her wouldn't have been fun for them. As they had long planned, they intended to subject her to the punishment they believed she deserved and had proudly reserved for her so they could celebrate their evil together as if they had won a trophy.

Like the demonic wolves they were, like the murderous wolves they had become, they ran without mercy or conscience to attack her. Their thirst for revenge and hatred drove them urgently to capture her. But the young woman heard them first, before they could get too close, and screamed in fright despite her limp, a result of her injured foot. She was emaciated from not eating well or drinking water, but fear overpowered her weakness. Like a wounded rabbit scared of being swallowed by a snake or a wild animal, her lame foot and malnutrition seemed not to matter. She started running through stones, branches, and sticks that hit her face, feet, and hands as she ran, sometimes falling but quickly getting back up, managing to escape from the furious, ruthless people and the murderous beasts chasing her. These wicked people wished to capture her alive just to torment her, as they said, to administer the punishment they desired, to hear her beg for forgiveness, mercy, and compassion, and to laugh at her heartily while looking at her body covered in cuts from the wounds they inflicted, her entire face and body drenched in blood. They wanted to bathe her in substances that would corrode her skin, breathe them in to destroy her internal organs, or force her to swallow them. Seeing her die slowly would be the perfect triumph for them to celebrate together with immense pride.

For the moment, the precious young girl managed to escape from the ruthless beasts chasing her. However, she saw that the woman accompanying her wasn't so lucky. She also ran, but fortune didn't favor her because she tripped over a tree branch and injured her foot, unable to run further and get to safety. There, where she lay crying in pain, those cursed cowards caught her. Instantly, they took pleasure in insulting and beating her. The brief time the cowards spent torturing and humiliating the woman gave the terrified young girl an opportunity to escape her pursuers and lose herself among the forests, ravines, and large stones that could shield her while fleeing, preventing her captors from torturing her as well, which was precisely what those cursed demons desired.

While the macabre individuals detained the poor crazy woman who accompanied the unfortunate young woman, the beautiful, defenseless young woman, falling, dragging herself, and standing up, moved further away from the ruthless pursuers. But the wicked ones used their radios to inform others to search for her, communicating where they were and where the young woman had escaped. Like wild beasts hidden elsewhere, they went to look for her. Others, who were at home asleep, were called upon and joined the hunt for the poor defenseless young woman. Dozens of men and women with machetes, weapons, knives, and sticks ventured into the night, ignoring the danger to hunt her down. Despite the darkness of the night and the challenging terrain of the stream, even the dogs couldn't catch up with her or follow her tracks. Like rats fighting out of anger and resentment at not catching her, their fury and drool fell from their mouths, frustrated at yet another failed attempt to devour their feast. The despicable cowards remained convinced that the demon protected her, already believing that the precious young woman was his lover, his mistress, and even his prostitute, which is why he took her to hell and hid her.

Their hatred, evil, and frustration were so immense that some even cried, shouted, trembled, and foamed at the mouth as if poisoned. They hit each other and cursed themselves. In their sick psychopath minds, they spoke of the precious young woman as if in a litany, saying she was Satan's mistress and prostitute, which is why he took and protected her so they wouldn't find her and make her pay for their wickedness. Drooling and seething with arrogance, they shouted whatever perverse thoughts came to mind, discussing them with malice among themselves.

Time and hours felt like centuries for those deranged individuals. Every minute felt eternal, and every minute that passed without finding the young woman felt like an eternity. Each passing second intensified their resentment towards the young woman in their diabolical souls, causing some men, women, and children to grow exhausted and injured from falls or difficult terrains in the darkness. Some didn't care about their suffering; their thirst for vengeance fueled their continued pursuit, even though fifteen women, more than twenty children, and eleven men had already suffered serious injuries and had to be taken to clinics or home for treatment.

Once again, they remained like true wolves, howling in hunger. Once again, the feast they desired had eluded them. They hadn't tasted the delicious blood of their prey on their palates. The heartless villagers of that ranch were dissatisfied, filled with anger and hatred for the beautiful young woman. Like rabid wolves with vulgar words, they cursed the beautiful defenseless young woman for not capturing her. They remarked again that Satan had saved her, never knowing if a divine force or truly Satan had rescued her because everyone claimed Satan always protected witches and saved them from the fire. Yet, she hid in a place where the diabolical wolves, despite searching, couldn't find her. The bloodthirsty wolves remained howling without their prey, but they were sure they would eventually find her, knowing she was nearby and would soon catch her alive, for that was their desire—to hear her plead for mercy, see her die in pain, and then burn her like witches.

In a way hard to believe, the scavengers' hunt was thwarted by the defenseless young woman, mocking them right under their noses, hiding where they never imagined. She laughed at them from her hiding place, and when they realized, they imagined the worst of her, claiming she had mocked them with a demon's smile. She entered their cage, and they couldn't understand or know how she arrived or climbed onto the roof of one of the houses of those searching for her.

Seriously injured from the blows she received while fleeing, she was able to save herself for that night and day. The beautiful young woman suffered tremendously from the heat, nearly dying of thirst and hunger. That's why, knowing she would eventually be found, she decided to leave her hiding place at dawn, stepping out of the den of wolves chasing her. Her life might no longer have mattered, but severely injured and barely dragging her feet, she walked through the darkest places, thinking only of picking flowers from the field to later, with faith or luck on her side, reach the grave of the old lady who had cared for her as a child. Though terrified of the wicked, malicious monsters, she knew they would not spare her life if they caught her there.

The divine force helping her intervened again, or as the heartless cowards who wanted to lynch her claimed, she was protected by Satan because he loved her, which is why he protected and cared for her, saving her several times from being mercilessly torn apart by the wild wolves in a cruel and malicious manner. Due to that foolish thirst for vengeance from the furious villagers of that ranch, they cowardly pursued the defenseless young woman, driven by senseless debts from their mistakes or beliefs, harboring immense hatred towards her with macabre and heartless intentions, charging her without the slightest compassion.

No one saw or heard anything. Nobody wanted to admit how the young woman tricked them again or how she escaped from the roof of that house. It seemed unbelievable to them that she had left after the homeowners found traces of her presence and showed them to other villagers. Nobody could believe how she got away without being seen or sensed by any dogs. They believed she had even bewitched the dogs so they wouldn't see or bark at her. The fact was that she left without them knowing, and everyone was left with the foolish idea that couldn't be erased from their minds—that the beautiful young woman was Satan himself, his favorite lover, the prostitute with whom he frequently consorted. This was why he cherished, helped, and protected her, allowing her to mock them. But they were very sure that the final day for the beautiful defenseless young woman was approaching, and wherever the demon hid her, they would find her, or even Satan himself would tire of her and hand her over to them.

What those evil monsters desired was about to be fulfilled. For the beautiful defenseless young woman, her destiny, her life, her suffering, or her curse of being born and arriving at that ranch, in this land of sadness, pain, and suffering, was something she was paying for dearly. Even her beauty, her smile, her kindness, were things that were fading for the few who knew and adored her. Her existence in this life was ending, cowardly being charged by the villagers of that ranch for a foolish debt they created against her, with her life.

It was a surprise for some of the demon hunters, the wild wolves of that village, but it was much better for the beautiful defenseless young woman, for they didn't realize when she reached the field and wasn't seen while picking flowers. Before dawn, some of the savage wolves patrolling the fields were still searching and guarding those areas. But the curse the lovely young girl always carried with her was that her life was in constant danger. She had just finished picking the flowers, but on her way out, those malevolent demons pursuing her spotted her. Like the savage wolves they were, they sniffed her out and, like hungry wolves, they went after her.

The beautiful, defenseless young woman was in very bad shape. Despite being wounded and weak, she heard them shouting as they approached her. Unconcerned about her health but fearing for her life, like a frightened little rabbit, she once again ran to escape from them. Her weakness and wounds, her injured foot, seemed not to hurt or bother her; her only instinct was to run from where she was because the wicked ones who wanted to capture her had already seen her. She fled without stopping, jumping over ditches and holes, avoiding large stones and traps set to catch her alive. She didn't step on any, as if she knew where they were, and this further enraged her pursuers. They shrieked like rabid rats fighting, swallowing their venom and pride, their desire unfulfilled, once again left wanting to catch her.

For many hours of that hot, sunny day, the beautiful, defenseless young woman kept running, crossing small paths and trails, dangerous slopes and steep inclines, jumping over bushes, dodging trees and branches that could hurt her, and crossing wire fences that almost tore her apart. Falling and getting up, leaping over large stones and fallen trees, hours passed, and though the beautiful young woman grew tired and wounded, she stopped only briefly to drink a little water from the streams because she had no choice but to keep running to save her life. She knew very well that if those psychopathic, criminal hunters caught her, they would have no compassion for her.

To those ruthless, cowardly killers, capturing the defenseless young girl alive was the best trophy, although sometimes they saw where she was headed, and others tried to get ahead to trap her. They didn't understand how she evaded them, but capturing her would be the greatest prize, the best triumph to celebrate in their lives, the best gift they could receive. Despite falling or getting hurt, the wildflowers in her skirt never fell or were left behind. Like a scared, wounded animal, she kept running so that the people of that village, turned into murderous wolves, wouldn't catch her. At times, in the darkness of that night that had fallen once again, she vanished from their sight. But they were true hunters, like the real wolves they seemed to be, catching the scent of her blood from the trails she left behind while fleeing. The expert hunters and their trained dogs found her again, but the dogs seemed uninterested, tired, lying on the ground and losing her scent. The dogs didn't seem interested in seeking revenge for something they weren't owed. But seeing the animals' lack of interest in finding her infuriated the demonic hunters further. Some even talked about wanting to kill the animals because they didn't care about catching the young woman.

The wicked, macabre hunters whispered that the defenseless young woman was indeed the true demon. With rage coursing through their veins and venom spewing from their mouths as they watched the trained dogs, who seemed to have no debt to collect, they lost interest in finding her. But the wicked hunters wanted to kill her, though they preferred to capture her alive. Like wolves, they could be heard from afar, shouting to each other where they spotted her and where she was heading. Communicating via cell phones or radios, they coordinated along the trails she walked and the paths she fled, setting traps, placing wires and lassos to trip or injure her. They set nets, dug trenches covered with branches and dried leaves to catch her alive if she fell into them. But it seemed as if she knew where these traps were, never falling into any. Like real hungry wolves, they pursued her, and the shouts and offensive words they hurled at the defenseless young woman echoed through the mountains, heard from afar, across the hills, rivers, and villages, like the howling of wild wolves.

Several more hours passed in pursuit of her, but they knew nothing of her whereabouts. No matter how hard they searched, they never found her. During the hunt, a man lost his life walking a dangerous path when he slipped and fell into a ravine, hitting his head and body. Several other women, children, and men were injured or severely wounded by the falls and collisions while chasing the young woman or navigating difficult, treacherous paths. Once again, they thought that Satan had saved her from being lynched, or that she was the demon herself, or, as was another accusation, like another litany, that she, the beautiful young woman, and the demon were lovers, which is why he didn't let them find her and mocked them. This is what they all thought, as it seemed that way. Once more, with the immense desire to quench their thirst for vengeance and the hatred and disdain they harbored for her, those wicked wolves remained wanting to capture her.

It was about to be dawn, but the beautiful, defenseless young woman still hadn't appeared. The wicked villagers thought that someone helped her—a powerful divine force or the demon protected her, or that he had taken her to hell. The people guarding the grave of the old woman, who had cared for the young girl when she was little, never saw her arrive or leave the flowers she had gathered on the grave. Exhausted by hunger and thirst, gravely wounded from the falls, she fell asleep from exhaustion on the grave, having fled from the cowardly, ruthless people of that village.

It was early morning, with the first light of dawn, when the pack of murderous wolves saw her lying over the grave of the old woman who had cared for her as a child. They were surprised when they found her there. Like the hungry wolves they were, they rushed at her, pulling and hitting her to get her to stand. Cruelly insulting her, they kept shaking her without mercy. But they felt and saw she wasn't moving—she was unconscious. Those who held her were scared, and in fear, they let her go. They realized she wasn't moving or breathing and watched her for a while, doing nothing or saying a word. Like hypnotized or robotic, they paced from side to side without knowing what to do, with no agreement on their actions. For some mysterious reason, without discussing anything, they left the grave, leaving her alone there.

By divine blessing or good fortune, the young woman, who was pursued and left unconscious, was found by the crazy woman from the town. Released by the wicked ones who had captured her, as if she already knew the truth, she went to the cemetery. Seeing the young woman on the grave, she believed she was dead, thinking the cowards had killed her. Frightened, almost crying, she approached her, shook her by the arms, and spoke to her, but received no response. Realizing she was unresponsive, she hugged her and cried over her for a moment. Then, continuing to talk to her, she thought the beautiful young woman was dead. Crying, as if the young woman could hear her, she said not to worry, that she would soon return and ask for help. Sobbing with emotion and sadness, she continued telling the young woman that everything was alright, urging her not to leave, to wait for her return. Struggling to rise, she nearly ran away, though it was still a bit dark, causing her to trip occasionally, almost falling. Ranting in anguish, she scolded herself but continued her path in search of help. Someone saw her, asked what was wrong, and upon hearing her plight, joined her. Together, they hurried away, leaving the young woman alone.

By divine blessing or mysterious intervention, the young woman's friends, returning from the city, passed by just then. It was as if they sensed something macabre had happened to the beautiful young woman. They weren't wrong. By divine blessing or luck, perhaps due to a divine power, it was fortunate that just as the crazy woman from the village reached the road with the other person, they spotted some cars approaching and signaled for them to stop. By miracle or another blessing, the visitors looking for the young woman recognized the crazy woman from the village. They veered off the road and stopped their cars. The crazy woman approached them, and others got out of the cars to ask what had happened. Crying, almost unable to speak from exhaustion and the long walk, she told them what was happening with difficulty.

The cruel news the woman gave was unpleasant. The young woman's friends, who used to visit her, became tense, scared, frightened, and cried in despair, incredulous at what the crazy woman had told them. Immediately, they got into their cars to look for her. Only a few minutes had passed since the crazy woman had left the unconscious young woman on the old woman's grave when they arrived and found she was no longer there. Extremely frightened, nervous, and agitated, they searched the entire cemetery, but she was nowhere to be found. They didn't understand what had happened. No one knew anything. They asked people passing by or already at the cemetery, inquiring about the young woman. Everyone said they saw nothing, so they agreed that some visitors would return to the city to alert the authorities. Other visitors, once it was daylight, along with the crazy woman and another person, asked everyone they saw if they had seen anyone take the young woman from the grave. They questioned everyone around, but no one knew or saw anything. Some stayed, while others accompanied the person they met, searching through all the villages for information on the young woman. Despite their investigations, they found no answers regarding her whereabouts.

For almost two days, the visitors and authorities searched for the beautiful, defenseless young woman, but despite their efforts and investigations, they knew or found nothing. They didn't understand how she disappeared or if someone took her away, as no trace of the young woman was found, no evidence that she was taken or eaten by animals. They asked in the same villages where people hated her, but they said they hadn't found her. Those who saw her at the cemetery said they didn't take her because some returned to search for her after those people came back, and since they didn't find her, they said Satan had taken her, suggesting they could find her in hell with him.

During those days, the young woman's visitors and the authorities investigated, while the visitors stayed with the crazy woman in the young woman's destroyed house. They observed that perhaps due to the tremendous nostalgia of losing the young woman, the crazy woman had become even more insane. Now, she went alone to pick wildflowers, walking to the old woman's grave. Some visitors followed her so she wouldn't be alone. The crazy woman cried at the grave, murmuring as if speaking with them, saying she would pick wildflowers and bring them there. The visitors who followed her approached and talked with her, and she told them that they were there together at the grave, which is why she visited and brought wildflowers.

Because of this, the visitors began to believe the crazy woman, thinking perhaps something mysterious had happened, that possibly the beautiful, defenseless young woman possessed some divine power, and that she had buried herself next to the old woman's grave. This was why they found no trace of her, nor any evidence of someone burying her. The grave's earth showed no signs of being disturbed, and there was too little time for someone to have taken her away and buried or hidden her elsewhere, as nowhere in the cemetery indicated someone had been buried at that moment.

The visitors went to the city and reported to the authorities, requesting an order to exhume the old woman's grave. They were laughed at and mocked, but eventually, they were authorized to exhume the grave. With the order in hand, they returned to the village. They all gathered with the exhumation order and sought the company of some religious figures to witness the exhumation site and receive blessings. When they met with the religious figures, they explained what they wanted to do and why. The religious figures listened to them and believed them, replying confidently that this could indeed be a miracle. Without hesitation, the religious figures accompanied the visitors to the cemetery.

After several hours, the young woman's friends, the religious figures, and the investigators went to the old woman's grave. The young woman's friends and the investigators all noticed that the soil of the old woman's grave had not been disturbed; it looked the same as all the other abandoned graves. However, they trusted the crazy woman and believed in her truth, so they started digging.

Sweating under the intense heat of the sun, which felt like burning gunpowder on the bodies of those surrounding the grave, the people burned under the hot sun while simultaneously breaking into cold sweats due to the tension of their task. Perhaps they feared finding her, or not finding her, but with great care, shovel by shovel, they continued digging. Skeptical, they conversed about their doubts of finding her, as they had never seen the earth disturbed or anyone buried in mere minutes beside the old woman's grave—the same woman who had cared for the beautiful young girl when she was a child.

After several minutes of digging the grave, nearly half an hour passed as if under frozen conditions despite the immense heat. The investigators, visitors, and religious figures all stood still, shocked by the incredible surprise they encountered. Next to the bones of the old woman's body, they found the beautiful, defenseless young woman. Her body was still warm, and blood was visible in her wounds, fresh as if she had died just moments ago, with blood still oozing from her wounds.

The people who found her climbed out of the grave to allow the religious figures to enter. When they touched her face and body to remove her, they felt her body as if it had just died. Carefully, they uncovered her completely and took her out to see her. The forensic investigators and religious figures confirmed that she was indeed dead. The religious figures blessed her. None of those present could believe it, but the religious figures confidently stated that it was a divine miracle happening before their eyes.

For nearly an hour, they observed and analyzed the young woman on top of the old woman's grave, pondering what had happened, even though they found no answers. All who witnessed the miracle with their own eyes prayed, asking for her soul's rest so she might find true peace in the afterlife, free from the curse she encountered on earth as just a baby. And so, just as she was, she remained in the same grave as the old woman. Together, the two stayed, as the investigators and religious figures decided. They didn't want to conduct further investigations, deeming there was no reason to continue. Therefore, they reburied the defenseless young woman so she could enjoy her new life alongside the old woman. Everyone wished for her to find immense happiness in her new life.

It is said that time heals wounds and scars, but for the people of that village and the surrounding areas, it seems untrue. They find it mysterious that on a day like that, her birthday, she arrived in the village. At just five years old, she was left entirely defenseless. On a day like that, she turned twenty, having spent fifteen years among them in the village. And precisely at twenty-five, she mysteriously died. The most mysterious and inexplicable thing for all of them was how they found her, buried in the grave of the old woman who had cared for her as a child. Was it a coincidence, or a powerful reason no one could explain? They all believe it was a reflection or remorse as punishment for the evil they inflicted on the beautiful young woman. Those who punished her carry this remorse in their conscience like a heavy cross that punishes them in their lives. They now understand their mistake, but they can't turn back time to ask for her forgiveness while alive. Some even cry when they remember what they did, blaming and cursing each other and themselves for the cruelty they showed her.

Everyone believes they were too cowardly in judging and condemning her for things she had no idea about. Because of the malicious tongues of a few, everyone believed in their wickedness or foolishness. They comment that if, instead of condemning her from the first day she was left alone at five years old, they had helped and protected her, or at least not ruined her life, she would be alive today. They wouldn't carry this guilt or have her death on their conscience. They believe it's like a disease they suffer from, a pain that bothers them in their lives, and no one can cure the suffering of their conscience. For them, it's a terrible agony they believe only death will alleviate.

The truth of this story or memory has lingered for years among the people of that village. Some who participated in the malice against the young woman still live there. Even those who have died carried the memory of that beautiful, defenseless young woman until their last seconds of life.

Since the authorities decided not to continue investigating, they never blamed the people for the young woman's death. In reality, she was never attacked. They only investigated how many people participated in trying to kill her and intimidate and beat the woman accompanying the beautiful, defenseless young woman. To compensate her, a court order was issued for damage to private property and physical assault on the woman accompanying the young woman. They were forced to build a high-quality house on the same site for the woman. The court even mandated that they refer to her as "the lady," allowing her to live there for forty more years, her entire life. Additionally, they must pay the church a monthly monetary amount for a religious figure to buy her food, medicines, and provide care in case of hospitalization, and for any clothing or footwear she needs for life.

The question that everyone who remains living continues to ask themselves stays with them: they ponder the truth of what happened. At the grave where the defenseless young woman and the old woman rest, the wildflowers she picked always bloom. No matter how often they are destroyed, they never cease to flourish. Now they are seen everywhere, even in places where she was pursued or hid. The flowers are as beautiful as she was, growing in the thousands. In memory of the young woman, these flowers are called "the flowers of the defenseless young woman." They named them so because it's a type of flower only found in that area. In other villages or cities, no one else has them. They say that even though many have tried to plant them in other places, cities, or states, they never succeed. Because of this, all the inhabitants of those communities and visitors from other areas or states are very surprised. Now, in their prayers at church, everyone is repentant. Some remember her with sadness, shame, and pain for what they condemned her for or when they saw her picking wildflowers.

The villagers of that village are sure they never knew and will never know if the young woman was truly guilty of what they accused her of or why they condemned her to a miserable life filled with hatred and evil. They continue to question what she was or what divine power she possessed, who helped her escape them when they pursued her with their insatiable thirst for vengeance. Why was it known that the commander and his two aides were violently murdered in jail just hours after the beautiful, defenseless young woman disappeared? They believe the same blessed power the beautiful young woman possessed was with them when they wanted to lynch her. In their minds, they never became murderers for killing her, but they feel guilty for their actions. They are now paying for the evil they did, haunted by visions of the young woman in their thoughts, dreams, and nightmares. When they pass through places where the defenseless young woman walked, they say they feel as if she follows or watches them. Some even claim to see her, the beautiful defenseless young woman, in the fields, the river, and all the places she used to walk when she picked wildflowers.